William Palmer is the author of four novels and a collection of short stories. For three years, from 2000–2003, he was Royal Literary Fund Writing Fellow at the University of Birmingham. He has recently taken up a part-time Fellowship at the University of Warwick. He lives in London.

THE INDIA HOUSE

The locals call it 'The India House', but they have little to do with the three women who live there: grandmother, mother and daughter. Upstairs, old Mrs Covington dreams of India and the days of the Raj. Her widowed daughter, Evelyn, watches obsessively over eighteen-year-old Julia. She has decided that the girl is to be kept in a state of 'innocence'. As little as possible of the modern world must intrude . . . But it is 1956. Mrs Covington may try to avoid the modern world, but she cannot prevent the arrival of two men, her son Roland, and her eighteen-year-old grandson, James. The fragile paradise the women have constructed is about to be changed forever.

WILLIAM PALMER

THE INDIA HOUSE

Complete and Unabridged

ULVERSCROFT
Leicester

First published in Great Britain in 2005 by
Jonathan Cape, London

First Large Print Edition
published 2005
by arrangement with
Jonathan Cape, part of
The Random House Group Limited, London

British Library CIP Data

Palmer, William, *1945 –*
  The India house.—Large print ed.—
  Ulverscroft large print series: romance
  1. Family—Fiction 2. Great Britain—History—
  Elizabeth II, *1952 – *—Fiction 3. Domestic fiction
  4. Large type books
  I. Title
  823.9'14 [F]

  ISBN 1–84395–927–5

Published by
F. A. Thorpe (Publishing)
Anstey, Leicestershire

Set by Words & Graphics Ltd.
Anstey, Leicestershire
Printed and bound in Great Britain by
T. J. International Ltd., Padstow, Cornwall

This book is printed on acid-free paper

To Lynda

PART ONE

PART ONE

1

Mr Iqbal lay in the roadway beneath the bedroom window. He had been there for several days. Had he been killed because he was a Muslim? She had never really had occasion to ask what he was. They were all either one or the other, weren't they? Then she was at the door downstairs. Then in the street, standing over his body, looking down. 'Was it because you were a Muslim, Mr Iqbal?' she asked. The head was encased in a moving helmet of black and green flies. He did not answer.

'There is only one God,' someone said in her ear.

Mr Iqbal shrank. She packed him awkwardly into a small brown suitcase and took him to the hospital in Calcutta. She was sure as their taxi drew up that it was the year of independence, 1947. But then her dream began to fall away, its details holed and the remnants eating themselves quickly, like lace on fire. In her confusion, she briefly thought that she must go and visit Mr Iqbal. Then she was awake, in 1956, and in England. The clock said half-past five. She kept the curtains

3

open a little in summer. It was quite bright outside already, but if it was anything like other recent days, it would cloud over before breakfast.

★ ★ ★

In the room next door to Mrs Covington, her daughter Evelyn dreamed that they were having another argument. Yet another in which the old lady's voice was calm and slightly mocking, and she herself screeched like a parrot. An endless stream of women passed by the kitchen window, staring in. One woman pushed her face right up against the glass so that her red nose and red cheeks were pressed to the colour of putty. The face grew, swelling, filling the whole window frame, the great pale lips squashing against the pane . . . Evelyn shook herself awake, rejecting the dream, struggling away from it as quickly as possible.

★ ★ ★

And in the next room, Julia, daughter of Evelyn Walters, granddaughter of Mrs Covington, was in India again. She could not see the face of the young man whose silhouette blocked the window, whose shadow

4

the huge moon of India cast forward on the wooden floor. It must be James, her cousin. 'We were talking about you,' she said to the dark form. He came closer. The window vanished. He stood over the bed. He bent down towards her. 'I haven't seen you since you were a boy,' she said. Then she turned in her sleep, and he had gone. She dreamed now that the high sun cast a sharp-edged shelf of shadow below the window and the white walls glowed with the red and yellow of the illuminated carpet. Her dream made a yellow-white lined blind come down from a thick mahogany roller to cover the window, and a teak and brass fan revolve slowly, suspended from the ceiling, stirring the air.

When she woke the first thing she looked at, as always, was the picture of the Indian soldiers on the wall. Their bodies were tall and straight in the splendid uniforms. Their eyes looked into hers, unblinking. They had no names, simply the legend *Soldiers of the Empire* on a little brass plate tacked to the frame. Were they still there, in front of that long veranda, now India had been lost? Their square, moustachioed faces did not look old. But the picture had been Grandmother's, taken, as she said, before the war, when India *was* India. They would never grow old. Neither would Dadda. He was forever stopped in that other photograph on her dressing table. The only picture of him in the house; the picture that her mother purposefully ignored whenever she visited the room. Julia knew that her mother came into the room when she was not there: opened books had been closed, her place lost; drawers had been pulled out, and then been pushed back slightly awry. Julia had taken to memorising just how things had been laid in the drawers, even leaving a folded sheet of blank paper that looked like a letter among her linen, and finding it very slightly out of place. Why did Mother do that? She never did it in return. Julia supposed it was because her mother had the power to do such things.

Then she heard shouting from downstairs.

'Julia,' came her mother's voice. 'Julia, are you awake? It is nearly eight.'

* * *

Evelyn waited in the hallway for her daughter to come down. She gazed back into the dining room. The sky had gone grey; this July was one of the worst for years. But she always took comfort from the sight of the breakfast table, laid freshly every morning. It gave a feeling of great continuity and safety. And they were safe. For now at least. The child,

6

Julia, was growing and changing. She was no longer a child, of course. It was most distressing that things had to change day by day, month by month, year by year. Evelyn had meant to explain the processes of life to her daughter. But it was all too disgusting. She had left the necessary things out in Julia's room to avoid what she called to herself 'the mess'. The child had had the necessary intelligence. What could her mother say to her that was neither immoral, nor sounded like some dreadful medical textbook? It was a pity that these things had to happen. It would be wonderful if your children could remain children. Of course it was impossible, but could not one, even *one* child, *her* child, be spared this onward rush of time, 'this theft of innocence'? What a wonderful phrase for Mr Henry to come up with. He was not quite such an old fool all of the time. They had been lucky in a way to get him as Julia's tutor. He had agreed with her, when Julia was twelve and they were first drawing up a plan of education, how fascinating it would be at least to attempt to keep a child innocent. Not from all knowledge, of course. But to give as pure an education as possible. Not that, he had gone on, they were safe in assuming that children are indeed innocent. 'A man,' said Mr Henry, 'is not a saint because he cannot do evil; on the contrary he must be a great sinner, at least potentially, to resist temptations . . . ' And so on and on — potentially — he would have gone, if she had not shut him up.

But, for the time being, they were safe. This house, embedded in its lawned garden, its hedges, its strange county of Shropshire, had hardly changed since she had visited it as a girl. Mother, of course, had withered slightly since, but she was still remarkable for her age. Rex had never been here. Evelyn's marriage to Rex had not been welcomed. When they had returned to England no invitation had been forthcoming, so Rex had simply never visited. That was comforting in a way. She had no memories of him in this place. What someone once called — what was it? — 'the filmy presence of the dead', there was no danger of that here. No favourite chairs, no views from windows on to him in the garden. She shivered, recalling the emptied wheel-chair in the house at Croydon after he had died. Now, there were just the three women in this house. Ah, and one elderly gentleman of little consequence. To be more exact — an old woman, a middle-aged woman, a girl, and a man who was not much of a man at that.

★ ★ ★

Julia, washed and dressed, came down into the hall.

Her mother smiled, quickly and bleakly, inspecting her.

The long thin fingers, wintry all year round with their red knuckles, plucked at the points of Julia's blouse collar, removed a tiny piece of lint, and the fingertips flicked down, straightening the dark blue pullover. She stood back and critically examined the brown stockings and square-toed black shoes.

When she was satisfied, she allowed Julia to follow her into the breakfast room.

Grandmother and Mr Henry were already in their places. They looked, almost, like an elderly brother and sister. Their faces were long and pink with large eyes, like shaved horses, and they bowed and nodded slowly to each other in grave, low conversation as horses do. Mr Henry's cheeks were a little more reddened by broken veins, his hair was equally white but stood up on end in a fine brush.

'You're late,' said her grandmother.

'I'm sorry. Julia was slow this morning.'

Her grandmother stared at Julia. 'When I was a girl and we were late we had to go without our breakfasts. Isn't that how it was, Mr Henry?'

Mr Henry smiled and bowed his head.

'Indeed it was,' he said. 'But then it was a fortunate child who had breakfast to eat.'

'Don't be Socialistic. It's too early in the morning for that sort of thing.'

Mr Henry smiled a little childishly at Julia.

'I hope,' said her grandmother, 'that you are not infecting my grandchild with any of this nonsense. The Socialists are idle and vicious.'

'They are also robbers,' said Julia's mother.

'We have little enough as it is,' said her grandmother.

'We are lucky they are gone,' said Mr Henry.

'But have they? The present lot is almost as bad. Pass the marmalade please, Evelyn. Before the war we had two maids and a cook.'

' 'How's the Empire?' That's the touchstone,' said Mr Henry. 'That is what the King said as he lay dying. 'How's the Empire?' '

'Which king?' Grandmother asked.

Julia pulled her chair a little nearer the table. It was large and heavy. All the furniture in this house was too large and heavy.

'King George the Fifth.'

'How on earth do you know? How do you know that's what he said?'

'It was in the newspaper. In a book review. Last year,' said Mr Henry.

'Hum. You and your blessed newspaper.'

'I think, if I may say so, that it was the war,' said Julia's mother. 'But for the war — '

'But for the war everything would have been fine,' said her grandmother. 'Why did that have to happen? It was perfectly ridiculous and totally unnecessary. But for that — '

Yes, Julia said to herself. But for the war they wouldn't be in this mess. Here. Now. In this particular mess.

2

It was ridiculous, Evelyn thought, to have no rank or title to call Rex by to others. You could think of and refer to your late husband as the Colonel, the Major, even, at a pinch, as the Captain — though that was a little vulgar this far after the war. But in no way, even as a joke, could you refer to him as the Sergeant. And, to speak of jokes, there was his Christian name, Rex. She had thought it so original and rather distinguished, until she discovered it was a family diminutive of Reginald. But she could at least say of him, while he was alive: 'My husband is not well. You know that he was wounded in the war. My husband was awarded the British Empire Medal for his wartime services.' And when he was dead: 'My husband died of injuries sustained in the war.' It was a refrain that she had learned by heart, like a line of poetry, until she believed it herself.

What Evelyn never told anyone was how Rex had incurred his injury.

It had happened in 1942; four years after Julia had been born. Rex was a sergeant in the Engineers. She nagged him constantly to apply for a commission; she could not belong to the company of officers' wives until he became an officer too.

Rex had been superintending the unloading of a lorry. Four Indian labourers, two on the tailboard, two on the ground, were manhandling a very large crate. It was too much for one of the labourers. His grip on the bottom corner slipped. His thin brown arms slithered and flailed, his knees buckled. The men above shouted that they couldn't hold the weight. The tilted crate began to slide down. It seemed to Rex to take a terribly slow time to fall, so that he was able to take a short run forward and to shout 'Hold on,' as the men on the lorry let go. Rex took the whole weight, his boots sliding helplessly under the tailboard so that the bottom edge of the crate toppled, crushing his pelvis.

Of course, it was all the bloody fault of the wallahs on the truck, the officers agreed. Good man, Sergeant Walters, but a bloody fool to get himself banged up like that trying to save an Indian. But this was the problem — had the sergeant acted to save the labourer, or had he acted instinctively to try and salvage some of His Majesty's war matériel? In his pain and delirium, Rex was not in a proper state to say. He had acted bravely, no doubt of that. And he had saved the coolie's life — at some cost to his. 'Bravery, certainly,' said the colonel, 'but is it deserving of a military honour?'

'It might show the Indians we care,' said the adjutant.

The colonel looked at him queerly. 'Might show them we care a damn sight too much,' he said.

The debate swayed here and there in the colonel's office. It was obvious that the man — what was his name? — Walters — the man Walters was finished — they must see what they could do for him at HQ. The papers were passed up to Brigade.

The admin wallahs argued that a military honour was hardly the thing in this case. The medical report said that he would be in a wheelchair for the rest of his life and that he would most likely be in pain all that time as well. What about the BEM? Well, not enough done really. A civilian award, then? But he was in the Army when the incident took place. He would have his pension early, after all.

The sergeant got, in the end, a commendation on his record, a wheelchair, and a thirst for whisky. The idea of the medal — the round, silver medal with the watered silk ribbon that had almost existed, that should exist in a properly conducted world — that idea had been invented by Evelyn as a consolation to herself. The wife Rex could no longer console with his words or body.

And words were what their neighbours heard through the thin walls of the semi-detached house in Croydon on the return of the Walters family from India. Or, rather, words distorted into male shouts and rumblings and shrill female retorts and the occasional sharp cry, not quite a scream, followed by sobbing, or silence.

So the Walters argued? Who didn't?

The rows went on and on, until the quiet wished for by their neighbours arrived unexpectedly one day in the February of 1950.

Evelyn Walters had been out shopping. The sky was the colour and thin furry texture of a grey National blanket. Snow, that had fallen freely in huge soft flakes two days before, now lay compacted in crusted shallow channels. The west wind had brought rain that morning and the rain had frozen immediately, giving a treacherous glassy top to the iced pavements and freezing at once on the small bare trees that grew in each front garden. The rain had frozen around each twig so that, when the wind gusted and the twigs clashed, tinkling together, ice broke off and littered the gardens and the pavement's inside edge with what looked like hundreds and hundreds of tiny broken bottle necks. Evelyn walked, her black hair tied back under a scarf, the wind reddening the dry skin of her cheeks and nose.

There had been another argument last night. But, as always, this morning she had helped Rex from the fold-up bed in the front downstairs room and into his wheelchair and counted out his pills for the day and brought a fresh carafe of water so that he could take them: all of the everyday, dispiriting routine. She could see by the way that his lips were drawn tightly in that this was to be another particularly painful day for him. Not for the first time she felt a sort of satisfaction at the thought.

But Rex had been strange when he got up. He didn't wince or grip his thighs as usual, trying to massage away the pain. The room was bitterly cold; the fire had barely caught yet, but he refused the tartan shawl over his legs. Just his sports coat, thanks, when he was in the bloody chariot. 'That's fine,' he muttered. 'That's fine.' His Engineers' tie. His breakfast on a tray, laid across the arms of his wheelchair. Then, settled, he was almost sweet, chatting about the old days in India. Did she remember the place he first

16

took her out to, the gardens at Jalipur? 'We'd just got a new captain, because Captain Cranshaw had had a heart attack on top of a native girl. They were in a single bunk and he was so big he'd flattened her and they lay there like that all night.'

She felt offended by the story, especially linked to their own early courtship. But she was more surprised by his smile, and the way he hummed some old song to himself as he propelled the chair to the window.

'Looks rough,' he said. 'Be careful if you're going out.'

'Are you all right?' she asked.

'Yes.' After a pause, while he stared out at the road again, he said, 'Has Julia gone to school? I didn't hear her go.'

'I kept her off. She's still got a cold. I told her she could stay in bed.'

'She should get out more.'

'The less she goes to that school the better. It will spoil her. She's already picking up the local accent.'

'We can't afford anything better. You know that.'

'We could ask Mother to help.'

'Ha. She'll never help you while I'm around.'

And again, this was spoken not with any of the usual viciousness, but with a sort of resignation.

17

'I must get to the shops,' she said. She went out to the hallway and put on her long black coat. She pulled on her gloves as she came back into the room. A tiny, brilliantly blue jet of flame spurted from one of the coals in the grate. 'It will soon warm up in here. Are you sure you are all right?'

'As I ever will be.' But this was not one of his usual bitter responses, such as 'It depends what you mean by all right.' And his eyes were bright in the livid snowy glare from outside.

'I'm going to the shops then.'

She was puzzled as she went out. She did not know how to deal with this new gentleness and resignation. What did he want? What was he playing at? She was usually glad to be out for as long as possible, but today she hurried her shopping. She went to the butcher's, and the general store, and it was still only half-past nine when she came out of the newsagent's, annoyed because she could not have her usual *Times*, but had to settle for the *Telegraph*.

She turned for home. For six years afterwards, over and over, she turned for home in her head. In six years her memory had grown a little less painful, but she could still not undo what she had found on her return.

18

3

A general system of Education: that was what Mr Henry proudly called it. A unique opportunity to educate the whole person in what could only be described as a wholesome way.

'Not for our pupil,' he enthused, 'the disease of modernity. A child, after all, is a blank slate, a *tabula rasa*.'

'I know what it means, Mr Henry,' said Evelyn irritably.

'Yes,' he said. 'Of course. So, the child is a blank slate which must be written upon, not allowed to drift willy-nilly on some meandering and whimsical voyage of 'self-discovery'. The purpose of education is to civilise the child, to introduce him — '

'Her,' said Evelyn.

' — or her, to the inherited glories of the Greco-Roman legacy, to Christianity or, rather, Anglicanism — the two,' said Mr Henry, 'fortunately do not always coincide; the Byzantine, Levantine, and, let us be truthful and say the *Semitic* aspects which are not always of the most wholesome; not to say the Papist, which may be regarded as a decline and deviation from the Byzantine in some lights — '

'Yes, yes; I understand,' said Evelyn.

'And also, of course, the child must master simple arithmetic, grammar, the *Golden Treasury, Our Island Story*, the Empire, the natural world — sticklebacks and things — but, I think, no later science. Science is merely confusing to the juvenile mind, and my own grasp,' he admitted, 'is rather superficial. Latin, naturally; no one can write English who has not studied Latin. French — regular and irregular verbs — enough at least to order a *chambre* in an *auberge*. Although it is my opinion that foreigners really should not be encouraged to talk in their own tongues.'

This was meant to bring his conspectus wittily and gracefully to an end, but Evelyn did not seem to get the point. 'Well,' she said rather grumpily, 'I hope you will not skimp on modern languages.'

Mr Henry had been in France during the First World War; the Great War as he still called it. Because of his school he had been made an officer. Because of his poor eye-sight he had never served at the Front. Supplies, administration; he had not come back changed from that war as others were. If they came back. Mr Henry thought the complaints

20

of the poets of that war a little overdone. After all, many of the chaps at the stores were straightforwardly patriotic. His preferred poets were of an older school: Housman, the Georgians, though some of those were tainted by the war. But at least they were before that charlatan, Eliot. Well, really, Mr Henry would say testily to younger colleagues, how could a man who wrote such stuff be anything other than a charlatan? A clever one, I grant you, he would say, in answer to their arguments. Time, he knew, was on his side. Were a thousand years of prosody, of melody and cadence, to be thrown away at the whim of an American bank clerk? Those few parents who knew anything of poetic or artistic matters were reassured by his cultural conservatism. He wrote poetry himself for many years. In the 1920s it had been regularly returned with no comment by the leading magazines of the day. True, he had published a few verses in lesser journals, but their acceptance only seemed to make more bitter his rejection by the others. He kept his composing to himself after that. Besides, it was not wise to appear too artistic in front of parents.

Mr Henry had been a schoolmaster for thirty years after the war; a good one he thought. After what was referred to as The Incident, it was put to him that in view of his age it might be wisest simply to retire on a reduced pension. He had been at his wits' end after six months. It was then that he had seen the advertisement for a private tutor in *The Times*. He had written a careful letter of application in his much admired *cancelleresca* hand. A week later, a reply came, signed Beatrice Covington. Could it be, she wrote, that many years ago her son, Roland, had been one of his pupils? Roland Covington? Ah, yes. A most fetching boy. Roland had suggested that perhaps Mr Henry might be interested in the position that she had to offer, as a tutor to her granddaughter. He wrote back that he would be delighted to visit and discuss the matter. A few days later he travelled north to Birmingham by train, changed, went on to Shrewsbury, caught a taxi to Mrs Covington's house, and had been here ever since.

A boy pupil would have been better, but perhaps a girl was a wiser choice. He had been here for five years now. The girl had grown into a beautiful young woman. The year before, when she was sixteen, she had gained a clutch of certificates in the state examinations. What she was to do now, at nearly eighteen, was another matter. He had never known a house so closed in on itself as this one. There was no wireless, no television;

the only newspaper that penetrated the house was *The Times*, which he bought in the village each morning. The mother, Evelyn Walters, did not want her daughter even to visit the village unaccompanied.

But Julia was no mere, educated wolf-child. She had been in India with her parents. As far as he could gather she had led a normal life until coming here. He knew that she was growing restless under her mother's regime. There would be trouble ahead. What worried him more, though, was what would happen to him now that, presumably, Julia's education was coming to an end this year? He had been happy here. His quarters were adequate. He had a large bedroom with its own wash basin. He was permitted to install his gramophone in the library, so long as he only played music there with Mrs Covington's agreement. He had become the sole conduit of news in the house; every lunch-time he conveyed the news of the day before, in bulletins he had learned to tailor to the prejudices of his audience. He himself was Conservative in politics, but not so far to the right as the ladies. It did seem to him unfair that the poor should be, well, poor — but that was hardly his doing, was it? And Julia seemed imbued with that regard for the underdog and downtrodden that usually afflicts young people. What a pity she had to grow up at all and so deprive him of his position. Sooner, rather than later, he might be joining the ranks of the poor himself.

Mr Henry became aware that he was staring at Julia across the breakfast table. She smiled across at him. He smiled back.

Mrs Covington rose slowly and with effort from her chair. She flapped a hand impatiently at Mr Henry when he tried to assist her.

He subsided into his chair. Was Julia laughing at him behind her napkin?

'Well then,' he said. 'We must get on. What are we to do this morning, Julia?'

'It is for you to tell, not to ask,' said Mrs Covington, making her way out of the room.

Mr Henry smiled again, at Julia, at Julia's mother, and at the back of the departing grandmother.

★ ★ ★

Mr Henry's curriculum was based largely on one set of dark blue bound books, which lined eight feet of shelving in the library. He never tired of telling anyone who would listen that it was assembled on the last occasion when it was possible to contain, albeit in an abbreviated compass, all of human knowledge in one work. Which work, which work? he would have liked his listeners to enquire excitedly. Alas, they rarely did. He would supply the information anyway. The great work was the *Encyclopaedia Britannica*. Not, he hastened to inform them, the rather bastardised, Americanised form later editions had taken, but the Eleventh Edition of 1911. The last occasion on which the world's greatest scholars gave a disinterested view of their subjects, untainted by modernism or fashion. It was like a great stained glass window, he would say. There was not much it could not answer that was worth answering.

In these volumes there was only benevolent, pre-Revolutionary Communism; psychology undefiled by Freud; no Fascism; no cataclysmic world wars. The Empire was intact. God moved in, perhaps, increasingly mysterious ways, but he still moved. Any direct reference to human sexual activity was almost impossible to find by however ingenious and filthy an enquiring mind. Mr Henry would cite the articles on Anti-Semitism, on the Negro, on Peace and point out how wrong they were in their optimistic conclusions, but how suggestive, how redolent of what the future *might* have held, of what alternative and vastly better futures even small alterations in history might have brought about. He would introduce such topics at the dinner table — if Mrs Covington was in an indulgent mood.

'Take the case of Europe in nineteen hundred and ten,' he said. 'The situation was one of such a finely balanced mesh of trade agreements and political treaties that it was thought impossible that any war could break out. It was simply against the interests of men everywhere. So why, I ask myself, should a world full of men of goodwill, why should such a world divide and fall so rapidly into chaos and bloodletting?'

'Well, surely the immediate cause,' said Evelyn, 'was the assassination of Grand Duke whatever he was, at — where was it?'

'Sarajevo,' said Mrs Covington. 'By an anarchist, if I'm not mistaken.'

'Exactly my point, Mrs Covington. All the work done by men of goodwill, from wise statesman to industrious trader, all undone in the twinkling of an eye by a madman.'

'Not mad, Mr Henry. They knew precisely what they were doing. And after two wars they are still about their business.'

'Quite. Quite. And indeed, if he had done this business now, Princip, he would have been treated as mad.'

'Princip?' Mrs Covington raised her eyebrows.

'The assassin of the Archduke Franz

Ferdinand at Sarajevo. That was his name.'

'Oh, I see. Would you pass the salt please, Evelyn.'

'What do you mean?' said Julia. 'How would he have been treated?'

'He would have been analysed and pondered over and pampered. They would have said that Freud's theory of whatever showed that he had had a traumatic childhood or some such nonsense.'

'Mr Henry doesn't like Freud,' said Julia.

'What do you know about Freud?' her mother asked sharply.

'Only that Mr Henry has such a terrific down on him.' Julia laughed.

'I should think so,' said her mother.

'What were the methods for treating lunatics before Mr Freud arrived on the scene, Mr Henry?' Mrs Covington asked.

'There were of course asylums, as now. And despite the reputation of the English for cruelty in such matters, as in the public exhibition and baiting of the mad at Bedlam in the eighteenth century, by the mid-nineteenth century many such institutions were surprisingly liberal in their courses of treatment. However, for the type of prisoner we are discussing, the criminally insane . . . '

★   ★   ★

27

Evelyn had stipulated that she wanted her daughter to remain for as long as possible in a state of innocence. Mr Henry agreed, but privately thought the scheme unlikely to succeed. He did not broach the subject of Original Sin to Evelyn. She said to him simply that she thought that the modern world corrupted the pure and that she wished to keep Julia away from that corruption for as long as possible, at least until she had learnt the old tried and trusted values. Mr Henry certainly agreed with tried and trusted values and he framed his curriculum accordingly.

So, History was British History. Even more specifically, English History. Wales and Scotland were rather outlandish long-conquered provinces; Ireland was split into two parts: a renegade South that produced poets and potatoes and a loyal North where nothing had ever been known to happen. The Empire was still almost intact. Evelyn insisted on a large part of these lessons being taken up by the history of the British in India. There was to her mind no other sort. Mention might be made of Mr Gandhi as a loin-clothed troublemaker and the anarchy that raged after Independence might be given a place. Julia should be taught that Hindu and Muslim cannot ever live at peace together. Evelyn was firmly of the belief that the day would come when the more sensible of the Maharajahs would, after a face-saving but bloody and deplorable interval, be more than eager to invite the British to return and once more take up the reins of government.

What of the rest of the Empire? The stories of early explorers. The opening up of the Dark Continent. Khartoum and Gordon. The gold, the iron ore, the diamonds, the ivory — all fruits of the White Man's Labour. The noble savage. The appalling habits of the black man. His naïve beliefs, barbaric religious practices, childlike nature. 'Do not dwell too much on the African man,' said Evelyn. No, of course not. Mr Henry had never met an African, as far as he knew. Some black troops had come through Catterick once but somehow he had missed seeing them. The tragedy of the Mixed Race. 'I don't think you need dwell on that either, Mr Henry,' said Evelyn. But England; England, Home, and Beauty. The white, winding lanes; the church tower poking above the newly made hayricks; the everlasting summer evenings . . .

* * *

Mr Henry shivered as the sun went in, darkening the room. This was almost the last lesson in July.

'Are you cold, Mr Henry?' Julia's voice was concerned. 'The weather's really not very good for the summer, is it?'

'No, of course not. But I think we shall break in a little while, if you don't mind, Julia.'

'May I finish the last verse?'

'Please do continue.'

Julia began to read again:

'But I would throw to them back in mine
Turkis and agate and almondine;
Then leaping out upon them unseen
I would kiss them often under the sea
And kiss them again . . .'

As she read he went away in his mind for a moment. He was by the sea as a boy and there was his cousin, Arthur, and they were leaning against each other in the dunes and he could hear his parents and Arthur's mother calling, calling for them and talking among themselves on the path above the beach, then calling again. And he could smell the skin of Arthur's shoulder. He could now . . .

'We would live merrily, merrily.'

She stopped. 'That's all of it. I like it very much. But isn't there something awkward about that line, 'Then leaping out upon them unseen'?'

'Yes. We will discuss the metre later, Julia.' The pain had come back in his side. 'I would ask that we might stop now. I have just remembered something I must do. Something most important.' He coughed sharply.

'You are all right, Mr Henry?'

She gathered up her writing book and pen. She turned back as she went towards the door. 'May I borrow this?' She pointed to his Moxon edition of Tennyson.

'By all means. We shall reconvene tomorrow.'

That pleased him, pleased him no end — the girl taking the book. He eased himself in the armchair. He felt a little better now she had gone. The pain had eased. He got up carefully. His kidneys hurt, his knees hurt; he really must walk more. He hobbled away to the door, across the hall to the stairs door, to the slow ascent to his room, his bed, his book.

4

The soldier strode from one side of the yard to the other. When he came out of the shadow of the wall, his hair flamed orange-red. He paced back deliberately. At every stride he stopped and pointed down, and the Indian soldier following him hammered a short stake into the hard red ground. Evelyn stood away from the upstairs window as the red-haired man, the sergeant, faced towards her. He hadn't seen her.

They were about to put up a tent or, more likely, to judge by the number of pegs going in, to make a large rectangle, a marquee. She crept back until she was almost touching the window seat with her hips, her left hand holding lightly to the cool wooden frame. The sergeant was short and disproportionately wide-shouldered, but he moved with grace in the pegged arena. And then he did look up in her direction, looking over his shoulder in the way people do if they think they are being watched. This time she did not step aside quite quickly enough. It was ridiculous. He had his hands on his hips, back arched a little, as he stared straight up at her. His eyes were blue, his face reddened by the sun, not browned. She felt herself blush. She couldn't now retreat like some stupid girl. Her hand inched up and released the catch on the blind. It fell between Evelyn and the brilliant day like a guillotine blade.

★ ★ ★

Her father's bank backed on to the yard that lay off the parade ground. She was in the office on the first floor. This was the room where she and Mrs Forrester and Miss Willoughby worked, typing letters, filing, and reconciling accounts. Because of some ancient enmity, the two older ladies had been unreconciled to each other for the past twenty years. When it was impossible not to speak they addressed each other in short, clipped phrases. For other communications they relied on querulous, mocking notes: 'I thought you had the red daybook. Have you?' 'I have only the blue and black ones, I cannot assist you.' 'Assistance I do not want. It would be a help if you could try and find the red daybook.' 'If you insist; the red daybook has fallen behind your filing cabinet. Thank you.' Mrs Forrester was a widow and Miss Willoughby a spinster. They could no longer afford to go back to England, so they remained, sighing but only rarely complaining, and then bitterly, about this alien land of India. They took turns to make the tea for Mr Covington, Evelyn's father, who was manager of the bank. Mr Iqbal the chief clerk was not included in the tea arrangements. It was assumed that he took tea alone in the outer office for religious reasons. He was an educated man, Evelyn said many years later at the dinner table at the Round House — but a little *babu*.

'I remember him so well,' said Mrs Covington. 'Your father swore by him, said the place couldn't run without him. I used to find him a bit pompous and I'm afraid I used to take the rise out of him. They did get so very *humourless* if they had education.'

'He's probably running the bank now,' said Evelyn.

'I don't think so. Surely he would be far too old. This is all of twenty years ago — just before your marriage, my dear. I don't know what happened to him. India swallowed him. There are so many people, one really can't keep track.'

Yes; her marriage. Evelyn's insanity, her father had called it. To fall for a sergeant of all things, when so many officers were available. To her father and mother that was quite unforgivable.

The morning after Evelyn had seen the sergeant in the yard, she was at her desk. There was a timid knock on the already open door. Mr Iqbal said: 'Miss Covington, there is a gentleman downstairs asking to see you.'

Knowing, as her mother had taught, that you must never show uncertainty or indecision in front of a native, she had said airily, 'Oh, that's all right. I'll go down.'

'Only, your father is not here at the moment,' he said.

'That's all right, Mr Iqbal. I can deal with it. Where have you left him?'

'The gentleman is at window five.'

She saw him through the dark green thin iron bars of the cashier's window. Or rather, the back of him; a thickset, red-haired soldier. The cashier slid off his stool when she stood beside him. That was all right, she said, she would see to this. He might go and get *char*.

Hearing her voice, the soldier turned.

It was all quite impossible. He must apologise, he said. He had seen her from the parade ground yard. He had assumed she worked here. He had found out her name.

'How?' she said. 'How did you find out my name?'

'One of the clerks,' he said. 'There are so few English girls here, it was easy.'

She stared out at him. Did she have what

35

her mother called the Covington Glare — the terrible look that her father gave over his glasses? Presumably not, because the sergeant did not blink or blush or hang his head. He smiled broadly and warmly and hoped he hadn't been too forward, but he had felt he simply had to make her acquaintance. His face was brick red, his eyes were very pale blue, his uniform was crisply ironed; his body filled it well.

Their voices had been kept low, but she realised that the clerks at their desks were looking at her. Their eyes were lowered immediately back to their ledgers.

'I really must talk to you.' His large hands rested on the counter.

'Please don't be absurd. Not here.' She remembered saying those words for years.

'No — of course not. Not here. But somewhere else?' he said.

'No.'

'Where?'

Behind the sergeant, one of the double doors to the street opened. Her father came in. He hurried through the wicket gate. A sort of warning wind swept through the clerks' bodies, their backs straightened and the steel nibs of their pens scratched busily. Evelyn didn't dare turn to see if he had gone into his office. An Englishwoman's voice rose from one of the other windows, saying, 'Well it was eight pounds, seventeen shillings and eleven pence. Please look again.' Then her father was standing at the cashier's position, soothing the woman customer, running his finger down the clerk's ledger, murmuring, his finger pointing at some figure.

'Well?' the sergeant said.

'Not now. Please.'

And her father, a self-satisfied expression on his face, was advancing along the line of cashiers towards her.

'You'll have to fill that in,' she said, grabbing a green form and pushing it under the grille.

As her father passed he frowned question-ingly at her but did not stop. The sergeant examined the form, puzzled.

'Is that all right? Thank you,' she said loudly and stepped away from the counter. She could see her father mounting the stairs to his office. She followed, and at the top of the stairs he beckoned her into his office.

'Who was that man?' he asked, settling himself behind the desk.

'Only a soldier. He wanted to open an account.'

'Shut the door.'

She closed the door; in the outer office Mr Iqbal pecked at an ancient typewriter.

'He was a sergeant, wasn't he? Sergeants don't have any money. They get their pay on a Friday and drink it by Monday. Besides, Mr Iqbal is supposed to oversee new accounts. You know that. It has absolutely nothing to do with you, Evelyn.' As always at work, his voice was cold and businesslike. 'Why on earth did you go down to the window?'

'He knew I was your daughter. You weren't in, so he asked for me.'

'Asked for you? Asked for you?' Then he said gently, as if to himself, 'Man was as red as a beetroot.' He raised his eyebrows. 'And he asked for you?'

'I told him about the bank.'

'You know nothing about the bank. Not on its public side.'

'I gave him a form to fill in.'

'Which one?'

'The green. The correct one.'

'Um.' He tapped the eraser-tipped end of his pencil on the desk in a slow, regular *tuc-tuc* sound. 'Half these fellows can't write their own names. I don't want you down on the floor of the bank, Evelyn. And I especially don't want you talking to soldiers. Do you understand?'

★ ★ ★

That evening, the sergeant was waiting on the other side of the street, directly across from the bank, in the shadow of a shop's awning. She mouthed silently, 'Go away. *Away*,' as her father fussed behind her, laboriously inserting keys into the three locks of the bank's doors. When he straightened up, she glanced round. The sergeant had gone. Her father took her arm and guided her to the Austin.

The next day a squad of Indian soldiers erected a white marquee in the yard. The white NCO commanding them was a tall, thin, dark man. She was surprised at how disappointed she felt not to see the red-faced sergeant. She sat down at her desk and the white canvas top of the marquee gently rippled now and then in the corner of her eye. Once or twice she got up to look out of the window. Miss Willoughby was away with one of her 'heads'. Mr Iqbal was downstairs. All at once, the sergeant swung into view round the back of the marquee, an Indian corporal half-running to keep up with him. The sergeant tapped each of the guyropes with a pace stick as he went rapidly along and the corporal scribbled on a piece of paper on a clipboard. The sergeant halted at the end and looked up at the bank. He saw her and had the effrontery to raise his arm and wave slowly in greeting, a broad grin on his face.

Almost involuntarily, she smiled back at him.

It came as a shock to her to realise that she was attracted to the soldier. That night she gazed long into the mirror. Her face was pretty in a way, but her nose was too sharp and her mouth a shade too thin. Overall, three years in India had not improved her. The longer she looked into the mirror, however, the softer her face appeared, the more becoming her hair placed like that, or this way, perhaps ... Her hands moved slowly about her head and face. What could this handsome, robust young man see in her?

She had had only one previous 'affair', as she called it ironically. That was back in England, three years ago, in '35. She had been twenty years old and working at an insurance company in the City. The man was a senior clerk. He circled about her for weeks. One day she arrived at her desk and found a small blue envelope placed in the centre of her blotter. A note said that the writer had long admired her. Oh God — 'from afar' — she thought, but the writer did not go that far. Would she do him the honour of perhaps accompanying him to a picture house — the choice of film naturally falling to her — or some similar entertainment? She might like to address her reply via the internal postal system of the company; this would 'avoid perhaps the mutual embarrassment arising from a negative reply'. The writer hoped that such a reply would 'not be forthcoming' but he would quite understand and silently withdraw his attentions. It was signed, Gordon Harris.

She had agonised over her reply. At last she scribbled a seemingly casual note — after perhaps ten drafts — agreeing to meet him. 'On a purely social basis.'

He appeared at her desk the following Friday evening. He was over thirty, she decided. He smelt of brilliantine and cachous and paper. He took her to the cinema, always the early evening show, several times. On their first visit they sat quite apart in their adjoining seats. She apologised quickly when her elbow collided vaguely with his when they stood to go. On their second visit she felt his thin damp fingers encircling her hand in the flickering half-dark. By the third visit he had attempted to kiss her, inexpertly, missing her mouth, his lips grazing her cheek, his scented breath unpleasantly warm in her ear. She was somehow both annoyed and relieved when his physical advances went no further. Indeed, after this, they retreated, as if he was satisfied with the small victories of hand and cheek in the back row. They ceased going out together by mutual apathy rather than by any dramatic

41

decision. When she next saw him out of the office, he was courting a girl with round black-rimmed spectacles and a plump bosom. He seemed a great deal happier.

★   ★   ★

Evelyn knew she would not get off so lightly with the sergeant. That is, if she should be so foolish as to let anything happen in the first place. And she knew that he would not be seen as at all suitable in her parents' eyes.

But it was strange, in retrospect, how inevitably things fell out. Two nights later she left the bank alone and waited for him to cross the street. She thought, much later, that we fall in love with what is available to us. In this subcontinent of India, teeming with its millions upon millions of automatically ineligible males, in this suburb of Calcutta with its small community of middle-aged officers with their adulterous wives and their half-caste girls tucked away in bungalows, of bachelor traders who were either too young or too old, and the private soldiers, pie-faced and bad-toothed, who caught unmentionable diseases from those other women and girls in the shanties in the town — what else could she do but fall in love with the one half-decent male at hand?

When her father learned of the affair he threatened to send her back to England on the next boat; her mother did not cry, but said disdainfully, 'A sergeant? Oh, I think we can do better than that, can't we?'

There were not that many places they could go and they were not yet sleeping together. The cinema was small and really fit only for Indians. The bar of the Fountain Hotel was the haunt of the cabal of white businessmen. The Club was out of the question. The Jalipur gardens could only be looked round a few times. How Indians like the young clerks at the bank amused themselves was a mystery it did not occur to her to try to solve. There were places where young white women went and a vast number to which they would never go. So it came to it that the only place she could decently take the sergeant to was her own home.

At their first meeting her father was gruffly polite, but not excessively so. Her mother was brisk and almost rude, but always drawing back from being openly insulting. She affected not to hear his replies to her questions or jumped in with some cutting remark.

'Where are you from, Sergeant Walters?'

'Rex, please call him Rex, Mother,' said Evelyn.

'Where?'

'England, Mrs Covington.'

'Well we all come from there. Where in England?'

'Gloucestershire.'

'Gloucestershire? Why? Are you a farmer?'

'No. My — '

'I can't think of any other reason to come from Gloucestershire, can you? Can you think of one, Alfred?' She turned to her husband.

'What?' He sucked at his dead pipe.

'A reason for coming from Gloucestershire?'

'My father was a printer,' said Rex.

'Oh, for heaven's sake, Mother . . . '

★ ★ ★

The meals. The walks. The drives, when Rex managed to get hold of an old Ford from somewhere. Meanwhile, her mother continued to put the good sergeant, as she called him, under her microscope. Had Evelyn noticed how prissily he held his knife like a pen; the suburban way he crowded food on to his fork in that infuriating series of little prods? How common his West Country accent was? And, in a way, Evelyn agreed with each fresh criticism. He was not well

44

spoken, though it was quite touching how his voice tried to improve over the tea table. She spoke to him once about his table manners. His face went puce and he swore terribly and jumped out of the Ford and stormed away. Of course, he had to come back to the car. He said thickly that he would try to do the right thing — but that her mother was a bloody bitch who meant him nothing but harm. It was her turn to rage. They did not speak on the way back, or for days after, until he sent a note, terse, but apologising if he had been at fault. She must be patient. There was only one way to resolve the situation.

In July 1938 they married. She was twenty-three; he was twenty-five. In November of the same year, to the scandal and amusement of the white community, a daughter, Julia Alexandra, was born to them.

5

Lessons, of a sort, had continued to the end of July. They had no real end in view now: Julia's mother was set against her going to university. Julia and Mr Henry were only passing the time together now. She waited for him in the room they called the library. One wall was completely covered with books; rows and rows in leather bindings, forbidding, unreadable. The collected works of long dead and forgotten writers; the novels of Mrs Henry Wood bound in green cloth; Hall Caine in blue. Dickens and Thackeray and Surtees and Trollope and Charles Lever, all solidly encased in leather. Two long shelves for Mr Henry's Encyclopaedia, another for his Chandos and Globe editions of the poets: Pope, Keats, Cowper, Goldsmith; the Moxon Tennyson. His French novels in browned paper covers, fraying at the edges. His Loeb Classics — and then volume after fat volume of bound copies of the perennially unfunny *Punch*. She longed to play the gramophone. She knew all the records by heart, but it would break the awful quiet of the place. She waited.

It was an odd house, seeming smaller on the outside than it was inside. In the village it was called either 'The India House', after the Indian rugs and pictures and odd items that the Covingtons had brought back with them, or, more commonly, 'The Round House'. The house was actually constructed as an octagon with eight wedge-shaped rooms downstairs, their doors opening on to the central hall. Side doors interconnected each downstairs room so that you could circum-navigate the house without re-entering the hall. Above the hall was an octagonal gallery, and off this were the six bedrooms, boxroom and bathroom. A glassed cupola crowned where the slanting roofs met and its light fell the whole height of the house.

The house was utterly silent. The french windows were a little way ajar but there was no sound from the garden. The door to the sitting room was shut. Behind it, Julia's grandmother would be doing, presumably, something. Sitting? Reading? Sleeping? What on earth did she do? What did she do *all* day? Julia wondered what would appear if you took an inventory of Grandmother's day — of any of their days, come to that. Precious little. Still, Grandmother was old; seventy-two. And through the other door, in the breakfast room, her mother would be sitting at the table, busily inventing and reinventing house-hold tasks for Mrs Fellowes, the help, to do when she came in at ten o'clock; or writing lists of future tasks in the house and the garden; sewing or embroidering or simply being a middle-class middle-aged lady of some leisure.

Julia's grandmother was forever saying that before the war a house like this would have had two maids and a cook and now they had to make do with Mrs Fellowes, who came in four days a week from the village. Presumably the maids would have slept in that plain whitewashed bedroom facing north. The room that had an old double bed in it with a stained mattress and, underneath, a battered trunk with railway labels. The room did not share in the ancient heating system that supplied the radiators in all the other rooms. Her grandmother said that it was the wicked levels of taxation of the Socialist government that meant they could no longer employ servants. The Government, she explained, would rather keep people idle. Well, they were all fairly idle in this house, weren't they? Julia reasoned. Her grandmother must be fairly well off, what with the tenant farmers and the money left by Granddad. But Grandmother perpetually reminded them both of the terrific expense involved in supporting them all and that, but for her, Julia and her mother would have to go back to that dreadful Croydon suburb. Well, Julia, for one, sometimes wished they were still there in Croydon. She could be with her father. No, she couldn't. She could only remember him; broad shouldered, his hands' vehement thrusts propelling his wheelchair round the back garden, bending over the side to snatch out weeds.

My husband is not well.

How many times had she heard her mother say that nonsense. Daddy had seemed very well, with his great ruddy face and powerful body. She knew he had been crippled in the war, but . . .

What had happened that day?

She had stayed in bed that morning. Her mother had come in early and drawn the curtains back. White ferns of frost were etched on the window against the half-dark world outside. Her mother had asked how her cold was. Julia said she didn't feel too bad. She might be all right for school. She'd missed two days already.

Her mother did not think she should go. In fact, she added, she wouldn't be at all surprised if it wasn't school that was making Julia ill so often. Some of the children, she said, looked considerably less than hygienic.

Why, even in India . . . For her mother the fall to this small house had been painful, as she frequently reminded Julia. England was not the country it had been before the war. The people living near them were not of their class. Julia was not allowed to play with the local children; she could not bring friends home from school. The school was a private one, but 'not good', as her mother said. It was in a large, gloomy house set beside a park. Every afternoon Julia would be picked up after school by her mother and they would walk quickly alongside the park's iron railings. From behind the bushes and trees came the calls and squeals and chants of other children. Back home, Julia would go upstairs to change out of her uniform of mauve blazer and black skirt. Sometimes she would steal into her mother's bedroom and look out at the road. Once, she saw a child watching her from the upstairs window opposite. The child was pale and had long fair hair parted down the middle; she was curiously small and her appearance faint and somehow oddly placed in the middle of that strange room. Then she knew, as the child across the way moved when she moved, that it was merely a reflection in a long mirror placed near that window. A reflection of herself, for no other child was so still, so alone. She befriended the image of the child across the road. She named her Juliana. Her birthday was on the day after Julia's own, so that the festivities could be extended privately. Juliana was a prisoner. Julia plotted her release. She wrote letters to her and detailed their conversations in a diary made from an exercise book. It seemed a betrayal when the light was left on in the bedroom opposite and the room was revealed. Then one day the mirror had been moved back into the depths of the room and all she could see was a pallid wedge of reflected sky.

On *that* morning — she lay in bed.

She heard her parents talking downstairs. She lay in that delicious, almost stuporous state that only a child in a warm bed, with the snow and day and school shut safely out, can fully and guiltlessly enjoy. There were old memories of India in her mind, but this too was a sort of India, this bed, warmth, sickness held at bay.

Her mother was down in the hallway. The front door opened. The front door closed. Julia sank deeper into the bed, her face framed by sheet and pillow and bedclothes. The sky between the curtains was grey and birdless. The thin top branches of their one tree were bare; some of the twigs made the rough shape of a six-pointed star. She began to be bored. She could read a book, but it meant getting out and padding over to the bookcase. There was no sound from downstairs. For a few more minutes boredom argued with warmth. Then she pushed back the bedclothes and eased herself out. She felt a bit giddy when she stood. She walked across the room and took down a book, and then another in case she didn't get on with the first. She knelt, her legs folded under her, taking a third, a fourth book from the shelf. The room was cold. About to gather up what was now a small stack of books, she heard her father call from downstairs. His voice was muffled. She opened her door. She couldn't see him. He must be in the sitting room door-way. His voice was magnified by the stairwell.

'Julia?'

'Yes.'

'Oh — you are there.'

'Of course I am.'

'I just wanted to know where you were. Why are you up? It must be cold in that room.'

He had never been in her room. He had never been upstairs in this house.

'Do you need anything?' This is what she had often heard her mother call down at night.

He did not answer tetchily, as he usually did. 'No, I'm fine. I just wanted to make sure you were all right.'

'Yes, Daddy.'

There was silence for a moment, then he spoke again.

'You must go back to bed. And not come down. Everything will be all right. Remember that and that I love you. All is for the best. Promise me you'll remember that . . . '

★ ★ ★

Mr Henry, hurrying into the room, interrupted her memory.

'Oh, my dear. I'm sorry I'm so late. So very late.' He put down his books perilously close to the edge of the library table. He had discarded the black coat he had worn to breakfast. The summer weather lately had been windy and rather cool and overcast; but today had started brightly and it was obviously in the hope that it would be sunny that Mr Henry had put on an elderly blazer of pale blue and yellow stripes with a heraldic-looking badge on the breast pocket involving a lion and crossed oars and a unicorn. For the rest, he wore a soft-collared white shirt and a bright red tie, brown corduroy trousers, grey woollen socks and open cross-strapped leather sandals.

'Where were we?' He snatched up the top book, glanced down his nose through his spectacles at the title and laid it aside. He repeated this process several times.

'Did you have the Tennyson? Thank you. *The Merman*, I believe. You liked it? Matthew Arnold also wrote a poem about these strange creatures. I've been hunting them down myself in literature for many years.'

For the next hour or so he talked about fishy and half-fishy literary beings; about mermaids and mermen, the Sirens, Poseidon, John Dory with the mark of St Peter's thumb on him, the Mermaid Tavern, Moby Dick, the Kraken, Grendel, the Deluge, the changing colours of the dolphin when taken out of the water, the Fisher King, Nereus and his seaweed hair and wife improbably called Doris, and about Neptune, Triton, and Proteus who lived in a cave and could change to any shape . . .

. . . and of some absurd moving picture he had seen recently where a mermaid was netted and kept in somebody's bath.

'Only an actress of course, with a tail fitted over her legs.'

'I wish I could go to the pictures,' said Julia. 'Why am I never allowed to go to the cinema, Mr Henry?' She held his eyes with hers. He glanced away in embarrassment. 'If you can, why can't I?' she said.

'Your mother,' he began slowly, 'your mother simply thinks that it would not be good for your education. She has your interests entirely at heart.'

She stared out of the window for a moment. The sun had gone again. Her lips half-parted as if she was about to say something. And then she said, 'Oh Mr Henry. What shall I be? What am I going to be when all this is over?'

Mr Henry looked puzzled. 'Well — you'll be a young lady.'

'What on earth is that, now, today?'

'Now is the same as ever, I'm afraid. The world is a difficult and frightening place. Your mother and I have tried to make your, ah, landing in it as painless as can be.'

'But this — ' She waved her arm at the books, the window, the garden, the high hedge, the church steeple poking above. 'This isn't the world. The world is India. Was India. And my father in the war and after, and school, and people — that's the world, surely?'

'The war is over, thank goodness. And India is gone, unfortunately.' He tapped the fingertips of his left hand on the closed Tennyson. 'Our glorious past — '

'That's just it. I'm sorry to interrupt, Mr Henry, but that's it, isn't it? I just want to know something about the future.'

'Well,' he sounded as if trying to be humorous. 'As I say, you will be a young lady. Then you will be an older lady and able to make your own decisions.'

'You mean I'll be like my mother?'

'Mrs Walters is an admirable — '

'Or my grandmother?'

6

Mrs Covington was seventy-two years old and sometimes she felt afraid.

Nothing was safe. Everything was safe. The house had been built in the middle of the eighteenth century by people who were no relation to her. That family had had it until the end of the nineteen twenties. They had evidently fallen on hard times and had to sell the property to Edgar, her husband Alfred's brother. The house was sound, but there always seemed to be something that needed doing, costing money. Edgar, wifeless, childless, died and the place passed to his brother in '47. Just in time; though Alfred hadn't lived to enjoy it much. The Independence of India, his own retirement, and the return to an England very different from the one they had left before the war had all been too much. She always said that that awful winter of '47 started the rot. Alfred's India colour had quite worn away, but a yellow tinge persisted in his face, lingering as a deeper shade in his sunken temples. He had looked forward to being a country landlord, but he had only sat at the rent table twice to receive the tenants' annual rents at Michaelmas. His cancer had taken him in the winter of '49. When all around the countryside had been made utterly silent and still by the foot-deep snow, his screams could be heard in the village; thin and distinct and distant, like a trapped animal's. He was buried in St John's churchyard, beside his brother.

Mrs Covington considered the rent table. She loved this table. It sat in the dead centre of the hall, which meant the dead centre of the house. Its top was an octagon of mahogany in the octagonal hall. The light from the cupola forty feet above fell on to its deeply polished surface. In each face of the tabletop was a drawer. One drawer was for the family; each of the others was labelled with a brass plate giving the name of the tenant farm: *Dickory, Crafold, Felldown, Wansdyke, Starcross, Tuckers* and *Dovestone*. Each of the tenants would come to the house on Michaelmas morning, take a drink of whisky or cider from the sideboard and place his rent in the appropriate drawer. The duty of sitting at that table once a year had become most satisfying to Mrs Covington. It was awkward receiving the money only once a year, but that was a tradition long written into the tenancy agreements. Of course, the rents were derisorily low, and her hands were tied in raising them by the iniquitous acts introduced by the Socialists. It was a godsend that Alfred's pension and savings had been augmented by the capital his brother had left. The price of everything had soared since the war, but these would just about do for the time being.

Like many people who are old but not yet senile, Mrs Covington lived what she called 'a busy life'. Evelyn came in most handily as an unpaid housekeeper for general purposes, and the child Julia helped out, but they could hardly be expected to do the washing and heavier cleaning. For this Mrs Fellowes came up from the village. So Evelyn had to be given instruction, and Mrs Fellowes had to be watched. Mrs Covington also liked to inspect the whole house regularly to see that everything was being cleaned and polished and dusted exactly as she wanted. Because the house was over-stuffed, this inspection could easily take two whole days. To Edgar's heavy Victorian furniture and imposing and dull paintings of Scottish landscapes, empty save for discontented-looking cattle, and Staffordshire dogs and shepherds and obscure generals on horseback, the Covingtons had added the ornaments and bric-à-brac from India. They had not been able to ship half of what they wanted and none of the traders wanted to buy anything back that they had sold you, of course; they had simply had to abandon what they could not put in their trunks. At first the Indian things had looked outlandish and alien in the Round House, but years had familiarised them: the brasses and ivories, the two small gilded paintings of a maharajah and his consort being carried in a palanquin by four servants in front of a stylised green landscape, first one way in the first painting, then the other way in the second, so that their mirror images forever approached each other above the mantelpiece in the sitting room. The Kashmiri bowls with blue birds and yellow and red flowers of a vividness never dreamed of in this county of Shropshire. The silver condiment set with menu holders in the forms of cranes, their long throats uplifted. All these, Mrs Covington reiterated constantly, gathered dust and lost lustre and must be kept up to scratch.

She had inspected the brass and silver this morning after breakfast and found them wanting. There really was no point in complaining to Mrs Fellowes; but she would make her point to Evelyn. What was the purpose in having a daughter in the house if she was not to be complained to? Anyway, it was eleven o'clock. Now was her hour for reading. She got her book and sat down in the bamboo armchair, facing the window in her bedroom. She was so still it hardly creaked at all.

She was reading, for the fifth time, *Sorrell and Son* by Warwick Deeping. It was a work whose philosophy she found in tune with her own. Mr Henry had agreed over lunch only yesterday that this was a characteristic of good literature; that it always found agreement among the greater part of its readers.

She read slowly the familiar words. Captain Sorrell was being sorely persecuted by his superior at the hotel where they both worked. How she longed for the moment when their positions would be reversed and the good Captain was shown in his true nobility. She read stolidly and slowly until, down in the hall, the long clock boomed twelve. She lifted her eyes and took off her reading glasses. Dust motes hung in the sunlight that came between the half-drawn curtains. She went over to the window. She could see the back of Mr Henry's outrageous blazer as he made his way to the gate. He had been Roland's housemaster at Cheshurst. A goodish school. What was to be done with Mr Henry? More to the point, what was to be done with Roland?

Her son's name was not often mentioned in this house. She had hoped he had settled down at last with that awful wife of his, Margaret — a schoolteacher, or something dud like that. And now the dowdy, dull Margaret had left Roland for someone else. It was ludicrous to imagine such a woman capable of passion. Still, she had probably tired of Roland's own excursions. Women will put up with those things so long as they are kept discreet and they can pretend they do not know. The whole nonsense was so important to men; heaven alone knew why they sometimes threw their lives away for it. Captain Sorrell had some very wise words on the subject for his own son. Something about it being a messy business, but necessary. Good for the Empire. Well, that was perhaps going too far.

Where Roland had got these urges from she did not know. Alfred hadn't been particularly keen on that side of things. After Evelyn had been born they had given up almost completely. And poor Alfred was not too well equipped for the occupation. Mrs Covington chuckled. Such small indelicacies presented themselves more and more to her mind as she grew older. She had heard of spinsters who, declining into geriatric decay, would suddenly unburden themselves of torrents of obscene words. It must need to come out in all of us. Thinking about it dispassionately, the Deeping thing, the conversation between the Captain and his son about women — that was rather odd for a man. Perhaps Deeping was a bit of an old pansy like Mr Henry. Julia should have gone away to school, but Evelyn had been set on this plan of educating her at home. Perhaps she was right. The schoolteachers were mostly Reds anyway.

But Roland had enjoyed his school, what with the cricket and rugby and all that sort of thing. A strong, handsome boy, he was always going to be in trouble with the ladies. There had been that girl when he was eighteen. That would have been in '30, five years before India. They were living in Wimbledon and Alfred commuted each day into the city. Summer, and Roland had had too much time on his hands. He had finished school and spent his days doing absolutely nothing. Then he said, absurdly, that he wanted to be a racing driver. That he knew some chaps who could get him a job in a garage. And the girl he met around that time was a common sort whose father was a milkman or something equally ridiculous. She had got into trouble — she was a good year or two older than Roland and should have known better. The atrocious mother had had the temerity to call at the house and to say that Roland was to blame. He had denied everything at first, then said that he was in love with the girl and intended to marry her. Quite impossible. Alfred was for putting him in the Army. Then he had arranged with his brother Edgar, and the boy had been packed off here, to the Round House, to cool his heels. The girl was placed in some home or other. Alfred gave the parents some money and they signed a paper waiving all future claims. Mrs Covington didn't know if there had been a child. Then Roland said he did want to go to University after all. They had hoped for Oxford or Cambridge, but really, without some strong family connection, it was quite hopeless. He had gone in the end to the Regent Street Polytechnic. People told her it was frightfully well known and brainy. She pretended it was the University of London. That was bad enough — but the people he had got to know. All arty, bolshy types. They must have been his downfall; he had left after only a year. Then, next, he was going to be a writer. She had not known whether to feel shocked or relieved when he said that he wanted to get married. He was not yet twenty-one. But he had a job of sorts, as a clerk in an advertising agency. Still, as Alfred had said, advertising was the coming thing, it was not simply a waste of time like writing.

So, Roland had married Margaret in '33. Their only child, James, had been born a few months before Evelyn's Julia. The cousins had not seen each other since they were small. Mrs Covington had not seen Roland for, what, seven or eight years? Then the letter had come this week, with the news that Margaret had left him. He had signed off that he would be in touch; 'James and I hope to see you soon.' The address was a hotel in Bayswater. What did he mean by 'soon'? She did hope he would not stay too long. It would be agreeable to see her grandson, James. She had not done so since he was eleven or twelve. Boys grew up so grotesquely after that. Except that Roland had never grown up. He had lost his wife and probably had no money. What if he wanted to stay? And stay. Mrs Covington did not look forward to the prospect.

7

Mr Henry felt frightened most of the time and he enlarged his fear by the exercise of his intelligence and imagination. Despite his almost Edwardian appearance — after all, some of his clothes were fifty years old and still fitted — he was not a ridiculous man. His tastes in literature and art, though long superseded in education and educated circles, were genuinely held. His truckling to the ladies' imperial fantasies and conservative prejudices was only partly insincere. He had long ago lost any youthful radicalism and like them he regarded the present and the future with aversion.

In the past few months he had felt the full terror of his situation. All of his life he had suffered from anxiety. This had been partly suppressed by the press of life, of work, the school, the boys, his own comparative youthfulness, but it was as if all that time he had been nurturing the real fear that he now felt in some dark corner of his being, somewhere out of the light of everyday life, somewhere that books and music and conversation never reached, the place where a man is on his own, stripped bare and defenceless.

And all of his life he had felt at the *edge*. In his youth he had felt sometimes as if he were about to make some wonderful discovery; that, all at once, the world would open and disclose its secret; that time and love and death would stand revealed and he would know what they were and how they related to each other and to him. At first, this was to happen through his own poetry. As Shelley had been visited, been swept, by the invisible wing of the very Spirit of Beauty, so the young Henry knew that the feelings he had were precisely as vivid, that his poetry would put him among the great. He never acknowledged that his thin lyrics were trite and worthless. He suspected that they might be, but never allowed himself to be wholly convinced. So, like countless other failed artists, he had become a teacher. At least, if he could not be among the great writers, he could disseminate their work among the young. His own work slowly died. For over thirty years now he had not been visited by that sudden beatific access of delight, the deceptive glimpse of some earthly paradise. What had cruelly replaced it were attacks of vertiginous fear. The feeling that he might at any moment step forward and fall into a bottomless abyss where there was no end to falling, no death even, simply a terrible *falling away* of the spirit, a madness where the mind held no other sensation than that — the endless, endless fall.

He stopped in the alleyway beside the churchyard, gulping in breath to steady himself. The sun shone on the green. He hurried inside the post office and bought *The Times*. He felt giddy still and went into the Bull. It was empty except for a pair of labourers in the public bar. He sat in the corner of the bar and drank two double brandies in rapid succession. He concentrated on the newspaper, and with the aid of the alcohol began to calm himself and to reassemble the Mr Henry who must go back to the house very soon and prepare the day's news.

★   ★   ★

Mr Henry sat at the desk by the window in his room preparing his report. He had been working since a little after half-past twelve. It was now a quarter past one; they must all assemble for lunch at twenty-five past.

Really, the ladies would be upset. News from the colonies was rarely good nowadays; the latest was quite dreadful. It was impossible to keep it from them. He anticipated their reaction. There had been that awful moment some years back when he had been idly comparing an old half-crown from 1942 with a new one from 1951, and wondered, in the idle post-lunch chatter, how long, given the parlous state of the Church, the words *Fidei Defensor* would remain on the coin and what would be left to His Majesty now that *Ind. Imp* had disappeared.

'In this house,' Mrs Covington had thundered, 'the King of England is still the Emperor of India.'

He tried to temper the news to their liking, but many things had to be mentioned, if only to be pleasurably deplored. Africa was of little interest generally. There would always be a substratum of discontent there, said Mrs Covington, as long as we, foolishly, continued to allow the native population to enter higher education. The movement to independence by some colonies was regarded as a tragicomic experiment bound to fail. Over the years there had been good news among the bad. The death of Stalin brought quiet satisfaction; an opportunity for Mr Henry to offer the opinion to Julia in one of their classes that such a momentous event might well lead almost at once to a complete change in the fortunes of Russia. Perhaps a full restoration of the monarchy, or at least a sensible conservative republic would come about. He had found in his room and brought to show her a book with a picture of the Tsar and Tsarina and their daughters and son.

'How beautiful they are,' he said to Julia. 'See how very beautiful they were.'

Julia's fingers travelled across the girls' faces. He told her how the family, the royal family of Russia, had been arrested by the Bolsheviks and taken away to a little town and locked up in a house with a high wall around it. He told how their boorish captors insulted and abused them.

'What happened to them?' Julia had asked.

They were prisoners, Mr Henry explained, but salvation was at hand. The White Army under Kulchak was advancing from the east. It would only have been a matter of days before the family were rescued and then who knows how the civil war would have gone? Or they might have been spirited away under the protection of the Royal Navy and been conveyed safely to England. But, said Mr Henry, their murderous hosts had told the family to gather up their belongings and be prepared to move. Fearing confiscation or outright theft, the young princesses sewed jewels into their clothes. But the only journey they were asked to take was to assemble in the cellar of the house. They had been ordered to sit on chairs, under the pretext of having their group photograph taken, no doubt. Then an officer and half a dozen soldiers had entered the room — men in dreadful baggy uniforms, with rifles made longer by bayonets, which shone in the lamplight. Some sort of proclamation had been read out, then the officer drew his revolver and shot the Tsar, and the soldiers had fired at the children and their attendants. And, as they fired, some of their bullets struck the rubies and diamonds and emeralds sewn into the princesses' clothes and sparked and ricocheted off. Could she imagine the horror?

The Tsar and Tsarina and their children stared out of the photograph. They stood, dressed in white in a garden. Behind them the few, high clouds in the sky had drifted into the picture, been frozen for ever on the exposed upside-down plate, then drifted serenely on.

'All dead, all dead,' mourned Mr Henry. 'But then — oh, so mysteriously — long after,' he said, 'out of nowhere, or rather Poland, out of the fog of history a woman appeared who claimed to be the youngest daughter, Anastasia. When her presumed killing took place she would have been about your age, Julia. A little younger perhaps.'

'Was she Anastasia?'

'*Is* she Anastasia? She is still living. Who knows? One would like so very much to think so.'

That night, Julia had dreamt that she was in a cellar that was almost like her grandmother's, but all the wine racks and bottles had gone. Mr Henry sat in one corner. He was agitated and trying to speak. She could not understand him. She looked down and was shamefully naked and then she looked again and she was dressed in a long blue silk gown. Some of the Indian soldiers were pointing rifles at her. They fired and they laughed when the bullets struck her and fell limply and dully to the floor. *It's lucky*, said a voice, *you have escaped*.

Later, she had told her dream to Mr Henry.

'Oh, my dear,' he said, trying not to laugh. 'Well, perhaps you are a lost heiress too. You remember that book we both read — *The Little Princess*? Ha. Yes. Indeed.' And to himself he thought, copybook Freud. No, that should be textbook Freud. And then he thought, how unworthy and mean it was of him to think like that.

There had been other good news, but it all seemed long ago.

The coronation of the young and beautiful Elizabeth had given rise to a rare alcoholic toast at the dinner table. Julia had been allowed a half-glass of burgundy. The bottle was brought up from the stock laid down before the war by Edgar Covington. Mr Henry kept a bottle of port hidden in his room, and occasionally replaced it; otherwise the bottles in the cellar lay dusty and largely untouched. And, generally, things had continued to decline.

Now this . . .

It was twenty-past one. He scanned over his notes once more. Then he went over to the wardrobe and drew out the port and poured some into his tooth glass. He drank it down in one, straightened his tie, patted his hair, and made for the door. As he went down the stairs the smell of boiled cabbage rose to greet him like a dank ghost from schooldays.

★ ★ ★

There were four of them, as always. Mrs Covington and Evelyn were already seated. Mrs Covington's eyes followed him to his seat. Julia flew in just as her mother was ladling out limp white-green cabbage. Last night's left-over lamb lay in grey slivers and small, irregularly shaped lumps edged with

73

white fat on a too large blue and white dish.

'You're late,' said Evelyn.

'I'm sorry,' said Julia mechanically. 'What's for lunch?'

'You can see what is for lunch. If you had helped prepare it you would have known beforehand.'

It was not, thought Mr Henry, an auspicious start to the meal.

Mrs Covington turned to him. 'Well, and what have you for us today, Mr Henry?' She began to chew steadily her first mouthful.

He smoothed his notes.

'The weather — ' he began.

'We know about the weather.'

Outside it had clouded over again.

'We do always begin with the weather,' said Evelyn.

'Oh, very well.'

'The forecast for the next two days is for a continuation of the present sunshine and showers, though with the likelihood of thunderstorms from the west.'

'We are in the west,' said Mrs Covington.

'From over the mountains,' Evelyn suggested.

They all began to eat again. Mrs Covington frowned at her plate, and then at Mr Henry.

'Is there nothing of any importance?' she said. 'It strikes me that nothing is ever

74

happening in your news lately. Is no one famous dead? No murders? No sex crimes?'

'Mother!' said Evelyn.

'Nothing lurid? Too much to hope for, eh? It's all very disappointing.'

'There is something, I'm afraid.'

'You sound very grave, Mr Henry,' said Julia.

He smiled as if with great effort and regret at her. He turned again to Mrs Covington.

'You will remember,' he said, 'my previous reports on the situation in the Middle East.'

'The middle east of where?'

He was slightly nonplussed by this.

'*The* Middle East, Mother,' said Evelyn.

'There is no need to be sarcastic, Evelyn. Mr Henry should be more precise in his descriptions. Carry on, Mr Henry.'

'It seems,' and it seemed to him that his voice had suddenly become resolute, almost Churchillian. 'It seems that, early this morning, the Canal Zone — that is, the Suez Canal — was seized by Egyptian troops and that the Egyptian leader, Colonel Nasser, has nationalised the Canal in the Egyptian interest.'

'*Nationalised!*' Evelyn's voice rose in a screech.

Mrs Covington was silent for a moment. She fixed Mr Henry with a terrible stare and then said, 'How has this come about, Mr Henry? From the tenor of your previous reports we hardly expected this.'

'It's hardly Mr Henry's fault,' said Julia.

'Be quiet, child. What do you mean, Mr Henry, by nationalisation?' Each syllable of the word was spat contemptuously and separately out.

'Well — in effect, in fact indeed — the gyppoes have simply seized the Canal. *De facto*, they are the possessors of the Canal.'

'Until they are evicted.'

'It is in their country, isn't it?' said Julia.

'I really don't know where your ideas come from nowadays, Julia,' her mother broke in vehemently. 'I hope, Mr Henry, you haven't included socialism and revolution in your courses?'

Mr Henry longed to say, *Madam, my courses are as pure as yours*, but couldn't rely on her complete ignorance of seventeenth-century English.

'Only in so far as they are dismissive of false theories.'

'What does that mean? Have you been teaching socialism?'

'No.' He feared he was beginning to sound ratty. He calmed himself. 'It is hardly possible to discuss modern history and entirely avoid — '

'I thought we said that we would exclude 'modern' history?'

'A contradiction in terms, I would have thought,' said Mrs Covington.

Mr Henry flashed her a grateful smile, but she ignored him.

'Why am I not supposed to learn these things?' said Julia.

'What has got into you, Julia?' Her mother was angry.

'I just think that perhaps I should have been given the opportunity to learn something of the world as it is.'

'Well, enough,' said Mrs Covington. 'It's a little too late to discuss all that. You have received the education your mother and I thought fit. It's unlikely you'll get another one now. I think at the moment that you would be better off making the custard for our dessert. It is apple pie, Evelyn, is it not?'

Julia's face was very red. 'I don't want any. Thank you,' she said, pushing back her chair and standing up.

'Well, we do,' said Mrs Covington very jovially.

Julia stood irresolutely behind her chair for a moment, and then went to the kitchen, closing the door firmly behind her.

'I don't know what you have been teaching the girl all these years, Mr Henry. It is just as well perhaps that her education is coming to an end.'

This time it was more painful for him to smile at Mrs Covington.

'However.' The word hung in the air. 'This is not the time. You were giving us this awful, awful news, Mr Henry.'

He repeated the details he had got from the newspaper that morning.

'This annexation,' said Mrs Covington. 'Like Hitler's of Austria. It is an essential waterway. The gateway to the Empire.'

'It is barefaced theft,' said Evelyn.

'You must keep us informed, Mr Henry.'

In the mirror on the wall behind Mrs Covington, his white hair flopped as he nodded his head. It was, he thought, like Gladstone receiving instructions from Queen Victoria; one old queen to another.

'Ah, pudding. Splendid,' Mrs Covington said loudly, as Julia backed in from the kitchen. She rather sullenly put down a pie dish with one hand, a jar of custard with the other.

'Pie, Mr Henry?' Mrs Covington asked.

'Ah yes. Oh good, good.'

'Custard?'

'I should say.'

And, during the solemn eating of the pudding, the three, Julia remaining silent, discussed the perfidy of the Egyptians.

8

I am a prisoner, Julia wrote on the inside back cover of her poetry exercise book. *Not in the sense that I am not notionally free to come and go. But where am I to go?* She had lived at her grandmother's house for seven years. She had memories of the school to which she had gone before that. Her mother told her that the school was no good; that she had not been happy there. Was that true? She would have liked to have become friends with a couple of girls, but her mother would not allow her to bring anyone home or go to anyone else's home. It would all have been different if nothing had happened to Daddy. Perhaps it was for the best that she had been educated at home. It was nearing the end now.

She had gone to school once more, when she had been taken into the neighbouring town to sit state examinations at the girls' grammar school. She had done well in her papers. English and Art and History were easy. Mathematics bore no resemblance to the arithmetic Mr Henry had taught her. Neither were there papers in his specialist subjects of Greek mythology, the Arthurian legends, Georgian poetry, Tennyson, Kipling, or sea shanties — which he bawled out in a surprisingly loud and resonant voice. Her French was good, though she delivered the oral session in the same English accent as Mr Henry used. He had said that it was vulgar and affected to speak French with a native accent. Latin she passed easily, though lately the lessons allotted to this subject had been filled instead with readings by Mr Henry from his favourite authors: Dickens, Jane Austen and Stevenson. When she became visibly bored he would read *her* favourites: *The Princess and the Goblin*, *Alice*, *The Wind in the Willows*. Mr Henry noted down, in his precise, beautiful hand, titles she had seen advertised in the backs of the old editions. Yes, he would hunt them down on his next trip to London. And, magically, he would always manage to bring at least one back with him.

Julia longed to go to London. 'You may go when you are of an age to appreciate it,' said her mother. That date had been set at eighteen; the birthday to come in November. The books she had devoured stood like visitors from London on the shelf in her room. So, that was what she had done with all the past years here — reading. And sometimes music, played on Mr Henry's gramophone in the library.

The one relatively modern piece of apparatus in the house, the gramophone had been brought here by Mr Henry. It had four speeds — 78, 45, 33, 16 rpm — and two needles to play the old or new records. Before that Julia had been restricted to playing Great-Uncle Edgar's collection of records from the twenties and thirties. They were mostly of music-hall turns, operatic arias by Melba and Gigli, or sentimental Irish songs by John McCormack. A few dance bands, with 'vocal refrains' by men who quacked like effeminate ducks. *The Laughing Policeman* was frightening in its unremitting jollity. For the rest there were songs from *The Mikado* and *The Pirates of Penzance* and some records of Ivor Novello — of whom there was a signed, framed photograph hanging behind the old gramophone. Julia was the only person who ever played Edgar's collection. Mr Henry brought with him dozens of records, of Beethoven and Mozart, Tchaikovsky and Elgar, Debussy and Brahms and a score of other names she had not heard of before. The music Julia now grew to love was that which Mr Henry saw fit to play.

She had never seen a television set. She had seen the picture of a film crew at work in a

81

book. She hadn't seen a film since — when? She must have been about ten. Long after they came back to England. She tried to remember. It had been with Dadda. But how had they got there without Mother? But he was strong. His shoulders were massive, the hands huge that moved the wheels of his chair forward. She must have walked beside him down that long suburban road to the white cinema that sat across the grassy traffic island. She had not been to the cinema since her father had taken her. Here, in the Round House, she thought, apart from a few quasi-modern amenities, such as electric lighting and the sometimes noisy and unreliable heating system, she might just as well have been living in 1856 as 1956.

The house and its rituals were almost all she knew, and she had been more or less content with them. But what she had seen of the outside world in the last couple of years had made her doubt the assumptions of the household and how it stood with that world. Surely all girls were not accompanied by their mother whenever they left the enclosure of the garden?

Every Sunday, Julia, her mother and grandmother set out for the village church for morning service. They dressed in black or navy blue; throughout the year they carried gloves. The two older women wore veils with their hats, and Julia wore a black pillbox hat that had been her grandmother's. Julia's mother frequently complained about the promiscuous mixing of the classes in the village church. In India, she said, there had been a very strict pecking order; the Indian Civil Service in the front pews with the senior military, then the junior officers, the lawyers and the bankers, then the buyers and jute brokers, then the clerks and other ranks. This social hierarchy was not observed so rigorously in St John's, although a pew at the side of the choir was reserved for Major-General Lowther and his wife. Mrs Lowther had called once or twice on Mrs Covington, soliciting money for charity, but there had been no invitation up to the Hall . . . 'Such snobbery,' said Julia's mother.

But really, what could they expect, Julia thought fiercely. The three of them dressed so oddly in their dark, old-fashioned clothes — she had heard the village girls gathered at the war memorial giggling as the three passed one summer evening last year, out for a walk. It was only this year that Julia had noticed the young men who came to church. They were the sons of farmers; young men with broad, sloping shoulders and thick red necks between their white collars and shorn, straw-like hair. One of them sat always across the aisle from Julia and grinned at her each Sunday as the women sat down. He had a round, sun-reddened face and as his lips peeled back she saw that his teeth were yellow like an old man's. What had these creatures, these Calibans, to do with the extraordinary raptures of love reported by the poets? Were these the instruments of desire and, God help her, pleasure? The mechanics of the sex act eluded her. She knew what she should look for, but the Encyclopaedia hid its anatomical references or mentions of reproduction in thickets of Latinate obscurity which, as far as she could make out, referred only to the lower orders of creation and left out their forked, hairy species altogether. Mr Henry had once left on the table a book about the Australian outback. But, even here, the photographs of naked Aboriginal males had been neutered, so all that remained in the genital region was an oddly fuzzed, empty V of flesh. Presumably something must happen between men and women to account for the poetry and for the picture of Michelangelo's David inexplicably uncensored in the Encyclopaedia. Perhaps not, though, because it was marble, not stirrable flesh. But the answer surely didn't lie with one of these ugly brutish young men. The choir sang lustily.

Julia stared upwards, to the high rafters that made the church look like the inside of a huge boat turned upside down and far from the sea.

★ ★ ★

Ah, the sea. That was one other place to which she was allowed to go. Once a year she and her mother went on holiday. Always to the same resort. It involved a long, tortuous train journey. From the local station to Shrewsbury. From Shrewsbury to Birmingham — that great, black city of nightmares. From there to London Euston. Then the slow, stopping train. The journey took all day. They left the dusty village and its surrounding blue hills in the early morning and met the Downs just sliding into evening shadow, and when they got off the train, they walked towards the sea as it lay like a great, gentle animal about to sleep, gathering the colours of the dying sky into itself.

They stayed always at Broadmere — a *private* guest house, as her mother put it. It certainly seemed private, as there were very few other guests. They always came well before the main holiday season and, apart from a few elderly couples adrift in the streets, or staring like imprisoned ghosts through tea-shop windows, the town was practically empty. The promenade had none of the cheerful clutter of chip shops and arcades and pubs of resorts further up the coast, but simply a line of white, ochre and pink four-storeyed frontages and gigantic, florid, deserted Edwardian hotels and scarcely smaller grand houses. When they walked out very early one morning before breakfast, and the sky was steel grey and a chill wind blew off the sea, the pale cold front reminded her of those lines from *In Memoriam* that had so terrified her:

And ghastly thro' the drizzling rain
On the bald street breaks the blank day.

Though the weather had been better for this year's holiday it had been, as usual, unutterably tedious. The round of antique shops, rain shelters looking out to sea, the trip on the small-gauge railway to Dungeness, with brambles scraping the sides of the open carriages, the marsh so desolate on either side — all this was so familiar that she thought they would find themselves imprinted on the scene.

Every year, on the second day, they went up through the town, up and up until they saw the sea over the rooftops.

'I wonder if it still holds Daddy's Army colours?' said Julia as they came to the military church.

'I should think so,' said her mother grimly.

Julia looked again at the stained glass window and its figure of a young officer killed in the First World War. The muted green and brown and blue of the glass let the light through on to the two women and Julia wanted to weep again for the poor lost young man. The banners of regiments that had used this church hung from the rafters and on the walls; some looked almost new, others had been faded and tattered by light and age. Julia was moved once more by the sight and she wished her father was with them and thought how fine he looked in his uniform in the photograph.

At Broadmere that evening, in the corner of the dining room, half hidden behind a newspaper, a young man was sitting over the remains of a meal. She would have liked to have spoken to him, if only to say 'Good evening', but her mother frowned at her as if reading her mind. The man got up and went out.

The next morning they sat for breakfast in the high-ceilinged, cream-painted room and waited for the girl to slap through the swing door to the kitchen. She came at last and took down their order laboriously with a stub of pencil. As she did so, the hallway door opened and the young man came in. He was dressed in a dark blue suit and a white shirt and an RAF tie. She decided that he must be a businessman, but then she thought that he looked too shy. His face was long and pale and quite finely boned. He nodded to them as he passed and sat again at the table in the corner. Perhaps he was a musician at the theatre, or even an actor. She looked down the room surreptitiously. She imagined sitting across from him at his table. Her mother shifted her chair to one side and said, 'Julia, do move round the table a little. I can't see through the window to the garden. A little more. More.' So that now Julia would have to look quite deliberately sideways to see the man.

He must have left the next day; they saw no more of him. As a treat, perhaps as a consolation, her mother took her to the little theatre on their last night in the resort. The place was only a third full. The piece was a thin farce, badly played. She looked for the young man on the stage, then around the audience. She thought about him on the long train journey home and later, as she sat in her room watching the evening fill up the garden between the high hedges.

9

The imminent dissolution of the British Empire cast the house into gloom. Evelyn went to her room after lunch, complaining of a headache. The headache was real, if a fairly low-level affair. She blamed the weather; overcast but warm, the air lying heavy. In reality, she simply wanted to escape to her room. She had her library books, novels by Hugh Walpole, Rosamund Lehmann and Dorothy Whipple, to get through. There was the darning of one of her mother's elderly cardigans; the thing was little more than a string of moth holes, but the old woman would insist that nothing must be discarded or thrown away. Rationing had been lifted, she would tell Mother wearily, and Mother would say, 'For now, Evelyn. For now. But wait until the Socialists are back.'

It was warm. Not hot. Not hot like India. Nothing was as hot as India. She lay on the bed and eased off her shoes. They fell with a satisfyingly plump sound to the floor. She laid her head on the fresh white lavender-scented linen pillow. She would sleep now. There was so much, and nothing, to do. She felt guilty at resting, but only that someone might discover her.

She dozed.

Then, once again, she was back in that winter, on that morning.

The road was black between mounds of mud-spattered snow. The pavement ice was rutted with footprints, scarcely melting each day and hardening once more each night. She was walking back home with a heavy bag in each hand. She didn't think of Rex or of her daughter. They existed at that moment, as she negotiated her slipping and sliding progress over the ice, only as a sort of buzz of undefined anxiety. Life was to be got through. Duty must be done. And seen to be done. Icy and seemingly endless was duty, like this endless icy pavement. The bags were heavy; a bottle of whisky for Rex was in one. He hadn't finished the old bottle yet, but she had bought it because of the gentleness there had been about him this morning, which had brought back memories of their first mornings together. Perhaps he was coming to some sort of reckoning with his physical state. God knows she had had to.

At last she came up to the house. The curtains were still half-drawn on Julia's window. The front room looked very empty and pale in the snowlight.

She opened the front door and stepped in. This is what she remembered always, the scene that recurred endlessly in dreams and from which she sometimes managed to struggle awake.

The front room door was open.

The kitchen door was too, facing her down the narrow passageway that ran beside the stairs.

Halfway along, the door to the small back dining room was shut.

She couldn't remember shutting it. Rex must be in there. She called his name as she passed the door on the way to the kitchen. He didn't answer. What was he doing in there? Perhaps he was listening to the wireless, though she couldn't hear it. She laid her bags gratefully down on the board beside the sink. Outside, the garden was filled with snow as if great sacks of it had been emptied roughly over the bushes and trees. Even the clothes line bore an inch of fluffy snow.

She unpacked her shopping. She put the whisky on one side. The rest of the packets and boxes went into the cupboards and larder. The whisky was to be a surprise. When she had put everything away, she picked up the bottle and carried it through. She tried the knob of the dining room and to her surprise the door wouldn't open. She tried it again. 'Rex,' she said loudly. 'The door won't open.' Now, from the feel, it was unmistakably locked. 'Open the door, Rex. Open the door,' she called again. She began to be frightened. From upstairs came Julia's voice, distant, muffled, asking if that was her, was anything the matter? Yes, of course it was her, and, no, everything was perfectly all right. Julia was to stay in her room. Evelyn realised that her voice sounded harsh and unfriendly and she was sorry for that but the child must stay put. What was she to do? She could not stand there hammering on the door and shouting his name. Part of her did not want to know why he didn't answer. He was asleep. He was drunk. He . . . In the hall mirror her face was white. There was a bunch of spare keys in the kitchen.

It took what seemed to be endless precious minutes to locate the keys at the back of a drawer, to hurry back to the door and then to fumble through them, trying one after another. The lock turned.

His wheelchair was facing the window. His broad back was to her. His head drooped forward, his right arm dangled over the side.

'Rex?' she said. 'Rex?' And she began to approach him. On the table beside the chair was his whisky bottle, empty. His bottle of painkillers, also empty.

'Oh, you coward,' she said very quietly. 'You coward. How could you? How could you?'

★ ★ ★

'Did he often drink in the morning?' Doctor Graham shut his black bag.

'I do not think I would express it that way,' she said. 'Often my husband couldn't sleep at night. Morning became his evening, if you like. So he would sometimes sleep later in the day. And these dark mornings . . . '

'It's hard to tell the difference,' said the doctor.

'He must have been confused.' She looked straight into the doctor's face.

'Yes, he must.' The doctor stared back at her.

He had been thinking about the whisky and the pills and the fact that the dead man had left no note. From the look of it there wasn't a lot of money. There might be some insurance though. It would not be kind to jeopardise the chances of that.

'He may well have taken pills early this morning, slept and then taken another dose with his drink,' he said slowly.

'I wasn't here for him to ask. That is the

unfortunate thing. He was a proud man.'

'Yes, he was. He bore a lot of pain.'

'What will happen now?'

'The undertakers.'

'There'll be no ambulance?'

'There really is no need. He was my patient. I've seen him recently. I can't see any need for a post-mortem.'

She felt as if they were talking in a detective novel.

'I really don't like to leave you alone like this, Mrs Walters,' he said. 'Is there anyone who could come in and sit with you — a neighbour?'

'I have my daughter here.'

'Julia?'

'Yes. She's upstairs. She's not well.'

'I'm sorry. All this must have come as a terrible shock to her. Would you like me to see her?'

'It's only a cold. I haven't told her yet.'

The doctor stared again at her. It was over an hour since he had been called. She had already said that she had had to go to the telephone box by the shops at the island. That was a slow walk in this weather. All that time the father had sat dead in his chair and the daughter had been in bed upstairs, knowing nothing.

'If you would like me to tell her . . . ?'

'I know my duty,' Evelyn had said frostily on that frostiest of days.

★   ★   ★

Mrs Covington had been in India for most of the afternoon. She had been looking through the old albums of photographs of life in Calcutta. How pitiable that they had to leave in those circumstances. And now, with this new trouble at the Canal, it was as if the anarchy and rebellion of India were flooding across the Indian Ocean, washing the coast of Africa and seeping through the strait.

The truth was that, when they had gone to India, they had been too old to enjoy it properly. Alfred had been fifty; she only a year younger. Even when they had first arrived, it had been made plain to them that they were not *old* India. She had been quick to realise what Alfred never did quite see, that the town, that is the English part of town, was a shimmering superstructure, solid enough in its bungalows and offices, but imaginatively a Little England, above and completely alien to the inhabitants of the all too real and concrete India of the Indians. Its customs and values intensified their emotional and material lust for what they had left behind, and what they were able to import into this place:

Keiller's Marmalade, the *Illustrated London News*, Pears' Soap and detective novels.

Chotu hazri, with Earl Grey tea and toast. Then Alfred would go off to work early before the heat and she would be left alone for the best part of the day — or longer, if he went to the club in the evening. It was not the very best club. That was for the ICS and the senior military. The social position of an area bank manager like Alfred was suspended between an inspector of police and the engineers at the Mills. The only thing she liked about the rise of Indians in the ICS during the war was the fact that it wiped the superior smiles off some of those faces. Good God, there had already been some Indians in Alfred's club when he had joined. Only guests to be sure, but they could still drink there. And when the war came they had to admit them as members too. And as for Evelyn's husband — well, she could not attend any officers' function and be accompanied by a sergeant. He was lucky to get an English girl of any sort, let alone someone of Evelyn's background. Most of the other ranks had to make do with Indian girls, for heaven's sake. Nice little crop of half-castes came from those liaisons. What was that appalling word for them that Alfred had picked up in the club? Anglo-Banglos, that was it. Or Eurasians, as the authorities called them. Whatever they were called, the poor devils belonged to neither camp, did they? An Indian of good family might be accepted in white quarters, but the Eurasian was not welcome anywhere. But the Indians were so polite that you never quite knew what they were thinking about you. And duplicitous too. Take Gandhi. A good family, wealthy, well educated — for such a man to pose as a peasant. And the insolence of Gandhi to say that the English would be welcome to stay on after independence. Did he think they had somehow become Indian, then? They were British, there to rule. Anyway, it was only the Gandhis and Nehrus who wanted independence. What good was it to the ordinary Indians? What good had it done them? Just as here now, in England, the clever Socialists, men like Gaitskell, were traitors to their class. Democracy, Mrs Covington conceded, was a fine thing as long as the right people were elected.

The war had been a grim time for the British out east, especially after the fall of Singapore. What if England too had fallen? Would not the Indians have looked at them and seen that the power of the English in the subcontinent was nothing but a gigantic bluff — a small man standing in the setting sun so that he cast a huge, long shadow. But if the sun set? Most of the Indian Army was, after all, Indian. The few British troops and police — what chance would they have stood against the millions and millions of natives? They had seen, at Singapore, that we could lose to people we considered racially inferior.

The war had ended it all really.

What was that thing that Churchill said? *This is not the end. It is not even the beginning of the end. But it is, perhaps, the end of the beginning.* That was after Alamein, wasn't it? The battle for Egypt. Well, he may have been right about that, but for the British in India it was definitely the beginning of the end. God, the brass neck of that American officer laying the law down in the club one night. Saying that the Brits were finished east of Suez. That there could be no going back to our old ways after the war. The sheer bloody cheek. And good old Porteus, from the jute mill, had leaned over and said quietly, 'Well, at least, old boy, we didn't have to wipe our Indians out, did we?'

Now this trouble at Suez. Where was that to end? They simply must take a stand against this new dictator.

And what was she going to write in reply to the letter from Roland?

PART TWO

PART TWO

1

He liked to be called Roly. Perhaps he was a bit old for such a boyish name; yes, perhaps, but still only forty-four. He couldn't say he'd had a bad life. A bit too soon to sum up, wasn't it? Like many men to whom the war had come as a release, he'd found it hard to pick up the reins afterwards. Or rather he hadn't wanted to be harnessed and ridden. He still missed the Army, oddly enough. There was something gratifying about being fed and watered and housed and paid — after a fashion.

The main road would give way soon. He would have to look out for the turning. The back roads were a nuisance. Pity they couldn't have afforded a better school for James. He should have gone to Cheshurst, but there wasn't enough money for that. It had all been a bit of a compromise. They'd settled on the Slate School in Devon because it was near to Margaret's parents — The Eternal Gardener and The Blue-Nosed Witch — so that James could go as a day-boy. 'That's Slate. Not Slade,' the headmaster had boomed at him in the way of somebody repeating the same joke for the eight thousandth time. 'Nothing too arty here. A good English education in the heart of Drake country. What could be better for a boy?'

Roland had thought at first that James would regret missing the experience of boarding. 'The only institution to which parents will queue up to send their children to be buggered, starved and beaten — and pay through the nose for the privilege,' as he said airily to Margaret. God, Margaret had wanted James to go to the local bloody grammar. What sort of start in life would that have given him? Perhaps he himself hadn't learned all that much at Cheshurst, but he had learned how to get on, how the world wags, how to be one step ahead of the other fellow. That is, if the other fellow hadn't been to Eton or Winchester, or one of the real schools. His friend Maurice Flatteau always said that he could tell a public school man by his voice, that he could even tell which particular school the chap had been to. There was a Westminster voice, an Eton voice, a Stowe voice. He had confessed himself baffled by Roland's accent. This had offended Roland, who prided himself on his slow, drawling voice. 'Like shingle moving on the beach as the tide withdraws,' as Margaret had said in one of those slightly baffling, but flattering, whispered remarks she had a habit of making in their early, intimate days. Well, she had been a poet of sorts. Poetess. Even published some in magazines. Too bloody brainy.

The turn was coming up. He slowed the Riley and nosed into a lane that was a green tunnel with trees either side meeting overhead and shutting out the sun almost completely. Very pretty she had been, Margaret. He had been too. He smiled at the road before him. Old Henry's rather breathless talk to them about the innocent beauty of the young. That was after poetry too. He had just read them Housman. *Blue remembered hills. Land of lost content.* All he could remember now. Bloody true, though. Inevitable too, in a way, 'lost content'. Move on. All he had left was the car. The flat was gone now Margaret had stopped paying the rent. Who would have thought it of her, going like that? He was the one who had the affairs, who should have made the hop to another woman. But no, off she'd gone, forty years old, husband and son left in the lurch, to go off with another chap. If you could describe Arthur Denniston as a chap. He had none of the essentials of chap-ness. None that were visible when he had come to the flat a few months ago. Surely they weren't having an

103

affair even then? He wouldn't have put Denniston down as the sort of man who would cheerfully consort with a cuckolded husband.

No, artful Arthur was rather small, perhaps seeming even shorter and slighter than he was through the timidity of his manner. Roland had seen that in some boys at school. They had suffered for it, for their difference from the robust norm. Arthur would have got it in the neck good and proper at Cheshurst. But, of course, the Arthurs of this world didn't go to school, they went to a school. Margaret had met him at a meeting of the poetry group, or whatever they called it, that met once a month in one or other of the members' houses. Roland had made damn sure, when it was their turn to host it, that he had given that evening a wide berth. So, Arthur? Like calling to like, he supposed. Margaret had, in the end, reverted to type, hadn't she? Grammar school, books, plain men with oikish voices — bound to happen some time. Personally, he could never take the Arthurs of this world. They might think they knew something, but Roland would rather have some of the ordinary chaps he'd had in the unit in the war. They weren't grammar school or any other sort of school. They despised and dismissed education as a mug's game. But they were filled with a vitality that fed off and flowed back into life, not some pallid, written-down version of it. Their lives were vivid, seize-the-day affairs. Knowing they might be killed any time made them live for women and drink. Before the war they'd worked hard in hard jobs and, when the war ended, and if they were still in one piece, back they went to their hard lives. But, for all their faults, they were better by a long bloody chalk than the Arthurs with their slim, damp hands and their books and their coward's view of the world. What else was it but a coward's view that saw such rough vitality as a looming threat? Roland's eyes pricked sentimentally at the thought of the men in the unit.

God, that group Margaret had joined. He had caught them once, at the end of their meeting. Opened the door of the flat and there was — what was her name, Avril? April? — some damned thing — but quite attractive in a mousy sort of way — reading some God-awful poem in a mournful voice. And they had all looked round at him and smiled — home is the hunter, indeed — the handsome husband of their hostess — that's alliteration for you, boys and girls — Mr Henry did teach us something — and there was the ludicrous Arthur, the only male in the herd, his face a boiled carrot red in embarrassment.

Then six weeks ago, Roland had come home unexpectedly early in the afternoon, to find Arthur, *seul* this time, on the sofa, and Margaret coming out of the kitchen, holding a Scotch in one hand and gin and tonic in the other. And Arthur had turned the carrot colour again. He'd assumed they were at some literary nonsense. Conversation had been stilted and had confirmed Roland's view of the man as a weedy nonentity. A view somewhat contradicted a week later when Margaret informed him that she was leaving, that she was moving in with Arthur, that the two of them were in love, that she wished Roland well, but — well, it hadn't really worked for years between them, had it?

The woman who stood before him seemed to turn instantly into a stranger. He examined her face — her eyes, mouth, hair — as if for the first time.

'You can't be serious,' he said.

'I've never been more serious.'

'Come on, Margaret. It's laughable.'

'Why laughable?'

'That chap — it's ridiculous.'

'You don't know anything, do you?'

'I know I've not been a perfect husband.

Who has? You knew what I was like when you married me.'

'We got married because James was on the way. And because I loved you. Then.'

'I . . . ' He stopped.

'Don't say you love me. You can say most things, Roly, but even you couldn't bring yourself to say that.'

'I did.'

'All right, you did. And some others along the way.'

'I never left you.'

She laughed, but coldly. 'You could never afford to.'

Ay, there was the rub. The play in his head came to an end. The car breasted a hill and for a moment he glimpsed the sea.

The severest rub — money. No, she wasn't going to pay the rent on the flat any more. Eighteen years and they'd never got out of those poky bloody flats.

In his head, they began to talk again.

'I suppose Arthur has a house. A nice little hice in Souf London. With a lawn. And a bloody bird-table.'

She shook her head slowly. 'There is nothing you will ever learn, is there?' she said. 'Nothing anyone can ever do to you, or try to show you will ever change you, will it?'

'What about James? He's just finished

school. He was coming home.'

'You're the one who wanted him to go to that absurd school. I love him. He's my son. But you've done such a good job on him.'

'What the hell is that supposed to mean?'

'You wanted him to be like you. Those schools are to turn out good chaps like you, aren't they? I hope they haven't succeeded. If you want any financial help for university I will of course help out with my share.'

'Your share?'

'Yes. And it will be given straight to James. I don't want it to go up in smoke on the 3.30 at Epsom.'

She had thought everything out. She had been packed and ready to go. All of her clothes and books and records had already gone that afternoon. My, they had been busy. He imagined poor, weedy Arthur staggering with piles of stuff down the two flights of stairs, then the front steps to the street. Puffing. Carrotty.

But, Christ, it was no joke really, was it? Not only had he lost her to that oik, but she had also left him completely in the lurch financially. He had only what he stood up in and the Riley. Well, there was a couple of hundred in the bank from that deal with Flatteau, but how long would that last?

So, like the Arab laddie, he had folded his

tent and stolen quietly away. He had rung Margaret's parents to tell them he would be picking up James. They could drive up to Driffold. Stay with Mother for a while. After all, home is where they have to take you in, isn't it?

Once more the sea came into view; perfectly blue, the tops of the small waves glittering. The place was further than he remembered.

2

James was getting ready to leave. His father had sent him a brief letter saying there might be a hitch but that he would come down in the next few days, certainly by this coming Tuesday, the 31st of July. Today was Tuesday. *Fact is, old son,* he wrote, *your mother and I are in the wars again and she's gone off in a huff. Not to worry, but it looks like us two against the world for a while. Ha. Be seeing you.* The signature was a huge, unreadable scrawl.

It was very different from his mother's letter. In five pages covered with her neat small handwriting, she informed him that matters between her and his father had reached such a pass that she could no longer go on living with him. She thought that James was now of an age where he could begin to understand these things. His father's frequent absences had not formed much of a basis for a stable and happy family life. *At one time,* she wrote, *I resented him being away and missed him greatly, but his conduct has led me eventually to prefer his absence to his presence. His continued rackety way of life,* his — let me be frank — many infidelities . . . It was best that they parted. She had found a good, kind man who wanted to take care of her.

I understand, she wrote in the final page, that your father has agreed to take you to your grandmother's in Shropshire for the summer holidays. Please write back and let me know if this is what you want. Unfortunately, my own circumstances are rather dependent on existing and long standing arrangements for the summer, otherwise of course you could have come here. Oh dear, it is all so difficult, but all will be well. All love, Mummy.

The letter had a tang of farewell about it.

James was in his bedroom. To be out of school was wonderful, but he no longer felt comfortable here. Sometimes, it was as if his future stood, a huge, irresistible, beckoning figure at each window of the house, at the doors and gate. But now he looked down out of the window, knowing that he would see only his grandfather in the garden. And there he was. In a woollen jumper, despite the warm air, he was, as always, doing something mysterious to something green and nameless. He wandered at all hours, from first light to light-exhausted dusk, among the flower beds, the hanging baskets, the arbours, the runner bean poles, the plum and apple and damson trees, the hawthorn hedge, and along the high, ivy-covered wall. He was like an elderly god who had to be constantly about his creation, for if he missed a day its precariously balanced life would fall into disorder, into unseemly green chaos. He had told James how he felt that everyone would quickly forget him when he died, and he didn't mind that, but that his garden, beautiful, but blind and callous, that *that* should forget him was the most awful of feelings. He did not mention James's grandmother in any of this. Perhaps he simply regarded her as a reflection of himself. Certainly, like many old couples, they had come to resemble each other physically. He was tall and very thin, his stomach concave under his stiff leather belt, his shoulder blades like nascent wings under the ever present woollen jumpers. And she was almost equally thin, allowing for the minimal curves and bumps due to her sex, and only an inch less in height. James found it difficult to recognise them from the photograph on the piano downstairs. The young man with thick wavy hair parted in the middle, his arm through his pretty, round-faced bride's arm. They were not simply his grandparents as younger versions of themselves, they were inhabitants of an utterly other world. It was absurd to believe that his grandparents had ever been young and handsome. James was eighteen this October — surely such very old people had never shared in his state? It was almost comic, and rather obscene to think of.

James regarded himself in the cool immortality of the mirror. His body, dressed in white shirt and grey flannel trousers, was lean and fit. His face, the tan pale in the white-painted, north-facing room, was handsome.

Behind him, reflected in the mirror, his suitcase was on the bed, its lid open, half-packed once more. He wouldn't be sorry to go. The place was becoming intolerable. His cricket bat leaned against the wall, its fate undecided. He had been quite a good batsman, but now he didn't want to hold on to reminders of school, of childhood and boyhood, of being a boy. Definitely to be left though were the stamp collection, untouched since he was thirteen, and the books of adventure: John Buchan and Captain Johns. But as he looked around the room, possibly — probably — for the last time, a lump began to form awkwardly in his throat.

He had, after all, spent six years in the place. But he had also been profoundly bored much of that time; stuck in the school terms in the long, dull evening of the elderly, accompanied only by the loud ticking of the clock, the clicking of his grandmother's knitting needles, and the distant chock-chock of his grandfather's spade digging, digging.

There had been breaks for the holidays, of course. There had been no holiday so far this year. With the new uncertainty about his parents he did not know what to expect. For the past few years, each winter and summer, he had been picked up by his parents. Their visit would be a short one. James's father avoided his mother-in-law as far as possible; her detestation of her son-in-law was plain. While the two women bewailed the fecklessness, stupidity and infidelity of men, he would chat to the old man in the garden. James would usually join them until it was time to leave.

Then, leaning against his suitcase in the Riley, he would be glad to be escaping back into the world, watching his mother flinch as his father once more accelerated round a blind corner.

The first holiday spent with his parents had been at a biggish house in Twickenham. By the next summer, that house had gone and he slept in the first of a succession of dingier and dingier flats. He grew used to hearing the arguments between them, through the bedroom walls. From his mother came the words, 'idle', 'drunk', 'unfaithful', 'filthy'; one tirade came to a climax with her assertion that he was 'just a conman. You're a crook and what's worse you're a bloody useless crook. You're not even good at that.' And all the time his father's voice, calmly intervening, his exact words lost in that murmuring, consolatory tone that drove her utterly wild.

Last Christmas had been spent in a large-roomed flat in Notting Hill. There was only one bedroom, so James had to sleep on a sofa whose springs were spread sparsely. When he laid his head on the cushion it smelled of musty tobacco and spilt alcohol and mice. But perhaps in deference to the fact that James could no longer be regarded in any way as a child, the outright rows between his parents were replaced by a simmering tension.

On Christmas Eve he lay down to sleep at half-past eleven. His mother had gone to bed. His father was still out. For a while he looked across the room at the small, artificial Christmas tree in the corner. The tinsel and baubles glowed softly in the light from under the bedroom door. He tried to sleep. He must have slept, for an hour had gone by when he was aware that the light was on again and that someone had come in.

''Lo, old boy,' said his father. 'Happy Christmas. Sorry couldn't come down the chimney.'

He lurched two steps to the gas fire. One hand was splayed against the chimney breast and his body bent almost in a right angle as his other hand snapped over and over at his cigarette lighter, getting no flame, ''Cause you see,' he said, giggling, 'bloody gas fire's in the bloody way.'

'Do you want it lit?' James said.

'Looks like it, eh.'

'I'd better turn on the gas then.'

'G' idea. So bloody cold out there. Sorry, I'm late. Am I late?'

James looked at his watch. Nearly one. He took the lighter gently from his father's grasp and lit the fire.

'God Christ, she'll kill me. Your mother will bloody kill me.' His fingers scrabbled in a bent and torn packet of twenty Senior Service. He got one in his mouth and, cigarette waggling, said, 'Have one. Have one yourself. Old enough now.'

'No thanks, I don't smoke.'

'What, don't smoke? Thought everybody smoked. Man should have an occupation.' He laughed. 'Oscar Wilde. 'Portance of Being Earnest. Saw the film. Damn funny.'

James lit his father's cigarette.

He drew in very deeply and expelled a long, satisfied sigh of grey smoke.

'Absolute bender, old Oscar. Scuse me. Is there still much of that at school, though? At it like rats in my day. Sorry.' He pulled a mock solemn face and then smiled broadly and inanely.

'But after all — bit too old for Father Christmas. And, my God, it is Christmas now, isn't it? Drink. What about a drink? There's some in there, get it will you, Jamie.'

The bottle of Johnny Walker on the sideboard had about three inches left in it.

'Glasses as well. Two.'

They sat either side of the gas fire.

'*Prost,*' said his father and tipped back the glass.

James took a sip and coughed as the Scotch burned the back of his throat.

'Present.' His father got up and made as if to step towards the sideboard, but then remained on the spot, swaying slightly. 'God. Must go to bed. Give a hand. Give a hand here.'

His father leaned into James, his body surprisingly heavy and firm. They went towards the bedroom door. There, his father halted and straightened his shoulders. One finger to his lips, the other hand on the door handle, he whispered, 'This far and no further, *mon copain*, my buddy. From here I must go on alone.' His laugh was high and silly.

The door closed behind him.

The living room seemed suddenly very bright and cold and empty. James went back to the sofa and sat down. Through the bedroom door he heard his father mumble something that ended with only one discernible word.

' . . . business.'

'Business?' his mother's voice repeated the word, weighting it with contempt.

So now, a long way from Christmas, he waited for his father.

What could he do until he arrived? His records were stacked on top of the chest of drawers. He could not even play them. There was no point unless you could play them loudly. And he couldn't do that, not after upsetting his grandfather this morning. About ten, soon after getting up, he had played, very loudly, a couple of sides of Jelly Roll Morton, then some Sidney Bechet. He had had the window open and, halfway through his recital, happened to look down. His grandfather, paused over his spade, was staring up at the window, his face unfriendly as he seemed to search for the source of the noise.

James stepped back. He was rather pleased he had upset the old man. He finished his recital as he always did by playing Bix Beiderbecke's *Singin' the Blues*. The pure beauty of the cornet solo, as pure as birdsong, aching with youth and love — that must make even the oldest and most cynical of men stop and listen in awe. As the record ended, James stole over to the window. His grandfather had resumed digging, back bent, eyes only for the breaking soil.

When James came down to lunch, his grandfather sat back with a smug smile, his upper lip drawn back like a senile wolf's over his upper dentures, and said, 'You like that nigger music, don't you?'

'I should think the whole neighbourhood heard it,' said his grandmother, knife and fork poised over her lamb chop.

'It's jazz,' said James indignantly.

'I know what it is,' said his grandfather. 'And you must agree that it is pretty horrible?'

'No, I don't.' He stared at his lunch. He felt as if something sacred in his life had been defiled.

'If you really must play it, do try and do so more quietly,' said his grandmother. 'It makes such a racket.'

The sun from the garden cast a green light

over the polished surfaces of the room so that it seemed half submerged. James had wanted to say that they were talking impertinently of the outpourings of genius. That they could know nothing of the beauty of this sound that had been unleashed on the world by noble souls. That it had nothing to do with their dreary wireless concerts of light music, their prejudices, their false teeth and spectacles and dust and dead books and little, wry remarks on this or that very *interesting* thing that had happened in the village today, or the nervous laughter with which they greeted anything they did not understand. That they could not possibly appreciate or understand anything loud and passionate . . .

'I'm sorry. I don't think I want any more lunch, thank you.' He pushed his plate away and stood up abruptly. To his surprise, salt tears pricked his eyes.

'Oh dear, temper, temper,' said his grandmother as he headed for the door.

'Temper,' said his grandfather, more savagely, then gave out that dreadful muffled, snuffed-out half-laugh they always used.

Why can't they even bloody laugh properly? he said to himself, recalling this for the fourth of fifth time upstairs in his room.

He lay on the bed. When would his father

come for him? The few birds of a summer afternoon twittered in a desultory way. He thought and thought of his father setting out from the flat, getting into the car, driving to the bottom of the street, turning left, round the crescent, then on to the main road, then to the South Circular. Then out, out . . . His breathing became regular and slow. He fell asleep. The noise woke him. He knew what it was. He jumped up and went to the window. He looked along the side of the house to the end of the drive, and here, the gravel crunching under its wheels, the Riley's bonnet came slowly into view.

3

'Something is to be done,' Mr Henry announced.

'I presume you mean this business of the Canal?' said Mrs Covington. 'Unless something still more terrible has happened in the meantime.' Mrs Covington relished the growing edge to her voice, her role, which she hoped would deepen with the years, as a sharp-tongued, indomitable old lady.

'I told you, I think,' said Mr Henry, 'that the Prime Minister has declared that Egyptian control of the Canal is totally unacceptable.'

'I thought he said 'single-nation' ,' said Evelyn.

'The Canal is *ours*,' said Mrs Covington.

'Of course, in a sense, and up to a point,' said Mr Henry. Mrs Covington sniffed. He went on, 'The Canal is *de jure* in the power of the Suez Canal Company, which though of course internationally owned is a commercial enterprise. Colonel Nasser has offered the shareholders some form of compensation.'

'The Canal is ours,' Mrs Covington said again. 'It is sheer piracy.'

'The English and the French — '

'Ha — the French. If we have to rely on them again, God help us.'

' — and the Americans.'

'Ha.'

' . . . all have deep political interests in the region.'

'Deep political interests. Deep *interests*, Mr Henry. The Canal is the gateway to the Empire. If this man Nasser is not stopped now, what will his next step be? Look what happened to our oilfields in Persia.'

'Grandmother,' said Julia, 'I do believe it's now called Iran.'

'I thought you were educating my granddaughter, Mr Henry?'

'Ah yes.' Mr Henry blushed. 'But on this point I fear the child is correct. No longer Persia, I'm afraid.'

'Doctor — I know not what he was a doctor of — Doctor Mossadeq, having become dictator of that country, then proceeded to nationalise our oilfields. Our Socialist Government, instead of defending our rights, withdrew our troops stationed there, and made the good doctor an outright gift of our priceless assets. Later that year, I remember it well, mobs of mad Arabs ran riot in the streets of Cairo. In the Turf Club ten Britishers were foully done to death.

Shepheard's Hotel — *Shepheard's* where my late husband had proposed a toast to the King only that year, Shepheard's was wrecked. The next year the King died. Surely these things shortened his life. I am sure they shortened your father's life too, Evelyn.'

'I know they did, Mother.'

'That is your *Iran*, your *Egypt* for you, Julia.'

'I know,' Julia said. 'I know terrible things have happened. Well, I don't know, not really. But in the end . . . ' She hesitated for a moment, then plunged on, looking from her grandmother to her mother and then to Mr Henry, saying, 'In the end they are not our countries any more, are they? I mean — we don't rule in those places any more.'

'That is the whole point, Julia,' said her mother, as Mrs Covington let out an exasperated sigh and lifted her hands in a gesture of despairing disbelief.

'We weren't always there,' said Julia. 'We left India.'

'We lost India.'

'We know this,' said Mrs Covington impatiently. 'Mr Henry, please continue with your report.'

Mr Henry gathered himself again. 'Well, yesterday, in the House of Commons, a Labour member, a Mr Paget, asked the Prime

124

Minister if he — the Prime Minister, that is — if he was aware of the consequences of not meeting force with force until it was too late.'

'The effrontery,' said Mrs Covington.

'If I might be so bold as to say, it might not be so,' said Mr Henry. 'In this case I think the remark was not intended ironically or impertinently.'

'The simple patriotism of the common man, you mean?'

'Precisely that.'

'Let us hope it was. This may be the turning point, but then you cannot rely on the Socialists.'

'Some served in the War Cabinet,' Mr Henry said timidly.

'Some. Preparing the foundations and scaffolding for socialism even then. If what this member said was meant sincerely, it is a good thing. But the policy of the Socialists to the Empire has always been one of 'scuttle'. That's what they do, they scuttle the ship, then scuttle off.'

Mr Henry and Evelyn laughed immoderately at this.

'What did Sir Anthony say in reply?' Evelyn asked as they regained their composure.

'Oh — good news. Matters have been put in hand most rapidly. Three aircraft carriers are to be sent to the head of the Canal. Other ships are to be directed to Middle Eastern stations.'

Mrs Covington nodded her head in satisfaction. 'It is all quite preposterous anyway, to think that the Egyptians would be capable of operating the Canal on their own — quite ridiculous.'

'Couldn't they prevent us from using it?' said Julia. 'Couldn't they just block it or something?

'They wouldn't dare,' said her mother.

'Now tell us something else, Mr Henry,' said Mrs Covington. 'Lighten our day with some good news.'

So Mr Henry told them of a foolish Welsh farm worker who had bought a new washing machine on hire purchase for his wife, although their cottage had neither running water nor mains electricity.

They all laughed at this, and Mrs Covington and Evelyn were heartened to hear of such stupidity still rife among the working classes.

* * *

That afternoon, Mrs Covington received a telegram. This was a rare event. The only people to come to the house were the grocer and butcher from the village and the postman with the occasional letter for the women, or a parcel of second-hand books for Mr Henry.

Julia answered the door to the boy and ran up to her grandmother's room with the envelope. It seemed to Mrs Covington that the girl was in a state of some excitement. To cool her, she took the envelope and examined it briefly then laid it on the bureau, unopened. The girl waited. 'It is, I think, addressed to me, Julia. Thank you,' said Mrs Covington and saw the excitement drain from the child. 'Oh yes,' Julia said, and turned away, disappointed and confused.

Mrs Covington heard her granddaughter's steps going down the stairs. She picked up her letter knife and slowly slit open the telegram.

ARRIVING TODAY WITH JAMES STOP HOPE OK STOP LOVE ROLAND STOP

Part of Mrs Covington was pleased; age and time had not quite erased her fondness for her first-born. As a child he had been quite delightful, with a handsomeness that could only have come from her side of the family. Her own mother had talked reluctantly and with distaste of the wild blood in their ancestors, the wicked great-uncles of family legend. Mrs Covington had never actually met any of them, and certainly dullness had descended on the family for at least one generation. She had been encouraged to marry Alfred, the bank clerk. Well, Alfred had been nice enough, but youth conceals with unlined faces and energy what age brings. And maturity had descended on Alfred very early. Roland seemed to have escaped all that, whereas poor Evelyn . . . Well, she had inherited the Alfred line; the only original idea she had had, and the worst, was to marry a common soldier. That, Mrs Covington sniffed, had presumably been *passion* at work.

Passion had not been a state that had bothered Alfred. Their own lovemaking had been lacklustre and dutiful. She doubted if she had ever felt the slightest physical stimulus from him. And what was he feeling as he dibbed and dabbed away at her every so often? That odd shudder, the expulsion of pent-up breath, the cessation of movement, the removal of the weight of his body, the disposal of those dreadful rubber things . . . what did all that mean to him? Then he would lie away from her on his back, then shift on to his side, showing his short, fat back with its one brown mole between the shoulder-blades. And she would lie there for a while, for quite a long while sometimes, staring at the ceiling.

They slept apart in India, 'because of the heat'. She could perhaps have had affairs out there, but Alfred did not move in the circle of people who had affairs. They were something you read about in prurient detail in reports of divorce proceedings in England. No, their generation had been groomed in the suburbs and villages of England for respectability and sacrifice and duty. Mothers of Empire. Well, she had produced her two for the good of the Empire and now it seemed that that generation was bent only on throwing it all away. The way they talked, you would think it had all been done for the most venal and ignoble of reasons. Did they think that they had done all this simply to subjugate inferior peoples? To steal their lands and produce? It was ridiculous — what had she and Alfred made out of Empire? They could have made a better living in England.

Roland had become infected with all these radical ideas in the Army. She hoped he had grown out of them by now. She looked at the picture of him she kept on her dressing table. It had been taken when he was eighteen or nineteen. So charming and feckless. He had always had a devil in him. Why he had married that schoolteacher or whatever she was, she could not think. People should have something devilish in them. Mrs Covington prized the devil in herself, it gave her endless amusement to let it slowly grow as she got older so that she might goad and manipulate the others in her little realm. After all, they all relied on her, didn't they? On her money, her . . .

As always when she thought of her money, Mrs Covington became disturbed. She pulled out the central drawer above the writing surface of the bureau. She drew it out entirely and reached her hand into the drawer hole. Her fingers felt around at the back where there was a shelf above the roof of the drawer. The fingertips met the bundle of papers hidden there, not as many as there had been, true; but still a source of relief and satisfaction. She drew them out. Her will, share certificates, birth, marriage and death certificates, all their details laboriously copied into ledgers and records and stored in the great institutions, in the pinstriped bowler-hatted Exchanges, held in solid steel and thick oak safety behind the classic columns of great banks and offices. How dare a bunch of dirty gyppoes think they could shake that security?

4

Julia saw them arrive. The summer evening was insistently alive still. She sat at her desk and saw the car turn through the gates. It halted below her window. Looking down, she saw only the tops of their heads. Two men, one young with springy brown hair, the other with a tanned bald patch showing through. The gates were rarely open; she had seen Mr Henry go down earlier and unlock them. The visitors must be expected. It was most probably they who had sent the telegram.

She went to her door and opened it softly.

There was a loud male voice in the hall; sounds were always magnified, rising up the deep well to the gallery.

'Evelyn. How very lovely. You got my cable? Hope we're not too much of a surprise?'

'I'm afraid you are a surprise. At least to me.' It was Julia's mother speaking; the surprise did not sound an altogether pleasant one.

'Sorry about that. What about a drink, sis? Bloody long drive up here, you know.' The voice floated up. It was a drawl, rather too much so in its sliding laziness. Julia stepped

131

forward to the balustrade.

'I cabled Ma.'

'Well that's no good,' her mother's voice dropped to a whisper. 'She never tells one anything. You know that.'

The two men stood at the rent table. The balding one, she knew now, must be her Uncle Roland, and the young one her cousin James. James stood a little way round the table from his father. The tips of his long fingers pressed against their own reflections in the highly polished wood. He had high, gawky, broad shoulders in a wheat-coloured sports coat, a white open-necked shirt.

Almost at the same moment, the two men lifted their eyes to where she was standing.

'Julia?' Roland's voice was very loud. 'Julia? It can't be. Come down, come down at once.'

In a moment she was down with them and Roland came towards her, his arms outstretched.

'Good God, Julia. You were a little girl when I last saw you. Come here to your wicked uncle.'

He embraced her. His cheek was rough; he smelt of brilliantine and beer. Over his shoulder she saw James straighten himself at the table, smiling nervously.

'This is your cousin James,' said her mother. 'Perhaps you don't remember him?'

A little self-consciously awkward in their movement, their arms and legs moving stiffly like two marionettes not wishing to become entwined, they met at the table edge. He raised his right hand to shake hers. She hesitated a moment too long and his hand was going down as she raised hers. And up and down once more, not coinciding.

'For Heaven's sake, Julia, just shake hands,' said her mother. 'James, go up and introduce yourself to your grandmother. It's so long since she's seen you.'

'Where is Mama?' asked Roland.

'Asleep, I shouldn't wonder. Resting before dinner. I suppose I shall now have to cook dinner for you two as well. It really is too bad she didn't tell me to expect you.'

'Where do I go?' said James rather nervously.

'Show him, Julia. Take him upstairs to Nanna.'

★   ★   ★

Mrs Covington sucked at her evening cigarette. She was sure that no one knew of this small secret vice. She sat in her bedroom, the window open to let in the song of the blackbird which perched each evening on the cupola. Beyond the garden she could see the church tower. The gold weathercock was on fire with the descending sun. The cigarette made her feel light-headed. She was glad when it came to an end and she could grind it out in the ashtray. She waved her hand to clear the smell of smoke.

She had her back to the door when the knock came.

'Yes?' she called out. She presumed that it was Julia come to say that dinner was ready. She heard the door open behind her. 'Yes?' she repeated, rather querulously this time. No answer; she craned her head resentfully round the high back of her armchair. Last light filled the white painted well. The figure of a young man stood in silhouette.

'Roland?' she said, and then was bewildered because he looked so young and lithe after his long absence.

'James,' said the young man. 'It's James, Grandma.'

★   ★   ★

The house and its inhabitants greatly amused Roland. The place hadn't changed a bit, except to look more dusty and dilapidated. His sister, Evelyn, had disappeared to the kitchen, complaining, once again, that he could hardly expect to treat the place as a hotel or canteen. He must send Julia into the kitchen to help her, when they all came down.

And now, here came his mother, flanked by her grandchildren, James and Julia.

'Roland. How wonderful of you to come — and after such a long time,' she said very loudly.

'Where have you been?' She came up to him and they embraced: his plumpness against her long bag of bones. 'And how James has grown. Julia, go and help your mother. Let us go into the dining room. Go ahead, don't bother about me. You know where it is.'

As she followed him, she said, 'I couldn't help noticing, as I came down the stairs, how thin the hair on the crown of your head is getting. Your father never went bald. You should wear a well-ventilated hat.'

And then, out of one of the many doors opening into the hall, Mr Henry came, rubbing his hands. 'I thought someone had come,' he said, 'but I hardly expected this. It is you, Roland, isn't it? If I may be permitted. How very good to see you.'

'Don't get in our way, Mr Henry,' said Mrs Covington sharply. 'We are on our way to sit down.'

So they sat in the dining room and Mr

Henry kept saying, 'Well, well.' And, 'This must be James.' And, 'It must be almost thirty years since I taught you . . . ' Until Mrs Covington shut him up rather sharply.

'Plenty of time for all that,' she said. 'Hasn't Evelyn prepared dinner yet?'

Mr Henry lifted his hands and let them drop to demonstrate a theatrical lack of knowledge of how things stood precisely at this moment domestically speaking.

'Well — go and find out. Perhaps that will shame her into feeding us at last.'

He hurried away, and came back a moment or two later. 'Another five minutes, I'm afraid,' he breathed.

The tablecloth was white, but bore the stains of several days' meals. Julia brought in a stack of dinner plates. Roland followed her with his eyes as she went out again. His son looked diligently down at his knife and fork.

'I am afraid you will find that we have grown quite slack and kitcheny since you last saw us.'

'Well, I didn't exactly bring the old dinner jacket,' said Roland. 'Though I seem to remember that you, Mr Henry, used to dress for dinner every night at school.'

'A school custom,' murmured Mr Henry and smirked at his old pupil, as if thanking him for remembering those glorious days.

'But men do look better dressed,' said Mrs Covington. 'Ah — food at last.'

The cold lamb left over from yesterday might have done for the usual four of them, but the few thin grey slices looked hardly adequate for six. They were supposed to fill up, Roland supposed, from the great mound of mashed potato and the dish of sprouts. The potato turned out to be thin and watery, the sprouts hard and bitter tasting. All in all, he thought, and allowing for the extra years she had to practise in, it was pretty much par for the course for Evelyn's cooking.

'Did you not make lemonade today, Evelyn?' said Mrs Covington.

'You know we only have lemonade on Sundays.'

'Ah.'

'Do you think — if you don't think this too revolutionary a question, Mama — but is there any chance of some wine?'

'Yes — wine.' Mrs Covington looked round the table as if searching for a bottle. 'Why did you not put any wine out, Evelyn?'

Evelyn glared at Roland, and then at their mother. 'But we never have wine.'

There was silence.

Mr Henry coughed. 'There is wine,' he said. 'If it is wanted. In the cellar.'

'Of course there is,' Roland said. 'Uncle

Edgar had tons of the stuff.'

'I don't even know if it's still there,' said Evelyn huffily.

'Well, it should be — unless you've drunk it, Evelyn,' said Mrs Covington triumphantly.

'Bravo,' Roland roared. 'Come on, Mr Henry. What say we get a bottle or two up?'

Evelyn shrugged her shoulders and sighed. Roland saw James smile at Julia, and Julia smile quickly back.

'Right, Mr Henry, lead on Macduff,' he said.

They crossed the hall to the cellar door and Mr Henry produced a bunch of keys.

'There's luck,' said Roland. 'Trusted with the keys to the wine cellar, eh, Mr Henry? No offence meant.'

'Please step carefully.' Mr Henry put on the light. The stone steps were narrow and deep.

'When I first came to stay,' said Roland as they made their way down, 'I must only have been seventeen or eighteen and Uncle Edgar always insisted that we drink a bottle or so at dinner, à deux. He was an absolute old rogue. I was astonished at how — '

Mr Henry switched on the lower light. A dull light, it showed the thick cobwebs on the bottles on the rack directly in front of them. But looking round it seemed to Roland that there were many fewer bottles than on his last visit some five or six years ago. Some of the bins were half-empty.

' — at how different from my father his brother was. Well, for a family that doesn't drink much, you've done quite well for yourselves.'

'It has been many years,' said Mr Henry.

'Evaporation?' Roland laughed.

The light just above Mr Henry's head gave his face an awful skull-like appearance, the eyes sunk back in shadow, the mouth like . . . No, Roland didn't want to think of it.

'I do seem to remember though,' he went on, 'that he laid down some Château Margaux in the late '40s. That should be more than drinkable now.'

'I think I know . . . Ah, yes, it was round the back here.'

Roland followed him.

'For a sober man you display a surprising knowledge of the contents of this place,' he said.

Mr Henry did not reply. He was bent over, feeling into the lowest rack. Puffing with exertion he pulled out a bottle, setting it gently down on the floor.

'I suppose we should have opened them for a while before drinking,' said Roland. 'I think we should have another, don't you?'

Mr Henry, who had been straightening his

body and coughing out dust, lowered himself again with a small groan.

'Do you remember those sherry parties you used to give us at Cheshurst? For what you called your 'brightest and best'. Were we? I wonder what happened to all of us?'

'Did I?' Mr Henry rose, clutching another bottle.

'Yes — you always had favourites. There was a lot of jealousy.'

'I'm sure I never had favourites in that sense,' Mr Henry wheezed. His face looked hot, his white hair was disordered, the white forelock falling over his brow.

'Right. Thanks for these,' said Roland brightly. 'I'll lead the way, shall I? Then you can lock up. If you think it's worth it.'

★ ★ ★

Two bottles were not enough.

The glasses fetched out of the sideboard had a fine sprinkling of dust and Julia had to rinse and dry them. After some debate between her mother and her grandmother, it was decided that Julia should be allowed a glass of wine. She looked so embarrassed that Roland laughed.

'Don't worry, Julia,' he called across the table. 'You're just like poor Sleeping Beauty, aren't you? But we've come to rescue you. Myself and handsome James. Ah, see them blush.'

'Really, Roland. You do talk such rot,' said Evelyn crossly.

In the time it took the women and James to drink one glass apiece, Roland and Mr Henry were halfway down the second bottle. The conversation had gone here and there. His mother asked Roland what he had been doing all this time.

Oh, this and that. He was in import and export at the moment. Big opportunities now in France and Germany. He elaborated on a whole, non-existent business concern. The office behind the Strand. The telex machine that you could type a message onto and send to the other side of the world in seconds. The maps of Europe and America with differently coloured pins representing customers and distributors and agents. The busy clacking of typewriters and the tick-tacking of office girls' heels in the corridors . . .

'But what do you actually make?' asked Evelyn.

'My dear sister — we don't make *anything*. You don't have to make things to have a business. We are facilitators, easers of the wheels of commerce.'

As he talked, he grew almost to believe in

the reality of this business. It sounded such a good idea. But he knew that good ideas and intentions never came to fruition with him if they needed the tiring and tedious preliminaries of actually putting them in place. It was far better to dream these things. He did not tell his audience about his real business ventures. The Cornish whisky — *Uisquebaugh Kernow* — two thousand bottles of tinted water, alcohol to taste, corked and lead foiled at the top. Fifteen shillings a throw. Or the Festival of Britain Special Passes for Privileged Guests, reply to this address, enclosing your remittance of one guinea. Rub shoulders with the nobs — never failed. The Swiss watches all the way from Swiss Cottage. Or the Coronation special issue genuine solid silver christening spoons, straight from the NAAFI. He had made good friends in the Army. A pity that the rackets had died away. That was the trouble when people became more prosperous. But Maurice Flatteau had come up with a good wheeze to cash in on the new industrial growth. It did sound a bit too much like hard work, though. You rented a factory somewhere, placed orders for goods — refrigerators, televisions, radios, washing machines — and paid for them up front until you'd got credit established with the suppliers. Then, one day, you hit them with a really big order on tick, had a bloody big sale, shut up shop and vanished. Thirty days' credit — you had at least a month's leeway before they even started asking ever so politely for their money, let alone before they started looking for you. Good racket, but you needed capital to start up. Same with cheap flats — you could live off the rents but you had to buy the places first. All the rackets in London seemed so far off. He needed a break anyway. Sandy Ferrers had got a bit too pressing in asking for that money back. Best to lie low here for a time, while he regrouped his forces. There might be something doing with Mother. So, stay for a bit. Bloody boring prospect, but okay.

Now a rather ruddy-faced Mr Henry was regaling them all with tales of Roland's schooldays. What an athlete he had been. Hurdler and sprinter, good off-break bowler and a fair batsman. 'Never, I am sad to say, what I would call a particularly good scholar. *Could have done better*, was the constant refrain on his reports. As well he could have, of course.'

'I remember the reports,' said Mrs Covington. 'I have them still. But, Mr Henry, you must agree that my son has not turned out too badly? This business of his?'

'It sounds very well,' said Mr Henry.

'But is it sound, Roland?' said Evelyn. 'In its trading and so on?'

'I am not too bad a businessman, dear sister,' said Roland.

'Yes, but to go back to my point — surely real businesses do need to *make* something. What you do — forgive me if I seem to be ignorant and stupid — but it all sounds rather intangible and impermanent, this moving of invisible commodities about. You never see them, do you?'

'Evelyn, I could hardly accommodate two hundred tons of coffee beans in my office,' said Roland. 'Or fifty Bokhara carpets. Even flying ones.'

They all, except Evelyn, laughed at this. Mr Henry laughed a little too heartily, so that he began to choke, and James had to strike him smartly on the back two or three times.

Roland waited until Mr Henry recovered, then went on. 'That is, if I may say so, a very old-fashioned way of looking at the world. The English have always been traders. That's what the City is based on. We were always brokers and middlemen. Believe me, the businessman of the future — his sole tools will be his intelligence and his chutzpah.'

'His what?' said his mother.

'Jewish word — for cheek, daring, chance taking.'

'Oh, the Jews,' she sniffed.

'Well, somebody will still have to *make* things,' Evelyn said, looking round as if everyone must now agree with her.

'No, I assure you, Evelyn, the other way is the future. You can make money from air, if you want to. You see . . . ' His hands described a huge invisible shape above the table. 'You say to someone that they can have this block of air, that it has been exclusively chosen and packaged on the side of — ah, whatever — of the Matterhorn, and that it is the purest, freshest, healthiest air in the whole world, so that, short of actually going and living up there, this is your only chance to own such a wonderful block of air and supplies are terribly limited and extraction costs are so high that it will cost x number of pounds — well then, someone will buy it off you.' He stopped suddenly, afraid that he had given something away, had let slip something that they shouldn't know.

'You sound very cynical, Uncle,' said Julia.

'Why so?' he said, and he was off again. 'It's what we do all the time. Only we call it religion, or the Army, or the Old School, or politics, or the Empire. It's all packaged air.'

'Don't be ridiculous,' said Evelyn.

'You can't see any of them,' said Roland. 'Oh, they all have adherents, members, soldiers, poor old devils like Mr Henry here.' He leaned over and patted Mr Henry's flushed cheek. It was damp and faintly bristly. 'They've all bought their two square yards of exclusive air.'

'Don't be ridiculous,' Evelyn said again. 'These things have reality. The schools educate the boys, the boys go into the Army, or business, or politics, and they serve the Empire and it all holds together. They are all the same thing . . . '

'As I say. Exactly as I say. Air.'

'Be quiet, all of you,' said Mrs Covington. 'Evelyn is perfectly right. You are being deliberately provocative. We have sat too long. It's almost ten. I am going to bed. Evelyn . . . '

'I am going to bed too.'

'Show the men where the bed linen and so on is in their rooms.'

'We're perfectly all right, Mother,' said Roland. 'I have been here before. I don't suppose things have changed all that much, eh?'

They all rose as Mrs Covington did, and remained standing while she led Evelyn and Julia out of the dining room.

'Thought we might go for a spin in the

motor tomorrow, Mother,' Roland called after her. She made her way across the hall towards the stairs without giving any sign of having heard him. Julia stood for a moment between the double doors.

'Goodnight,' she said and smiled, almost exclusively, it seemed, at James. Then she shut the doors to.

'Thank God for that,' said Roland, but quietly. 'Now, Mr Henry, how about another bottle. Or better still, where are you hiding the whisky?'

5

Mr Henry did not appear in the morning; neither did Roland. Grandmother, Mother, and cousin James — hair brushed back, in white shirt with sleeves rolled up — sat at the breakfast table. They waited until ten minutes past nine, and then Julia was despatched from the breakfast table to find out what had happened to the men.

It was exciting to have this male element present in the house. The dead place had come alive, thought Julia. You couldn't really think of Mr Henry as being — or ever having been — *male* in that sense. In what sense? In the way that Uncle Roland and James looked at her. They had completely different ways of looking, of course. Roland looked at her in a rather awful way and said sly things, like Sir Mulberry Hawk in *Nicholas Nickleby*, and not at all like an uncle should behave. James was rather sweet in the way that she sometimes caught his eyes on her and he would quickly and shyly look away.

She knocked on Mr Henry's door first.

There was no answer. She waited for a moment, then tapped again a little more forcefully. Did she hear something? Something like a faint moan, almost like a muffled sheep's bleat.

'Mr Henry?' she called. The moan came again, rather more vehemently, as if expressing pain. Julia was worried. Perhaps she should summon help from downstairs. That would look very weedy, particularly if there were really nothing wrong with Mr Henry.

She turned the door knob gently. One idle summer afternoon, years ago, soon after Mr Henry had come to the house, she had tried the door while he was out. It was locked. It was always locked behind him. But, passing by once or twice, she had caught a glimpse of the room as he backed out, key in hand. She had the impression that it was filled with furniture, pictures, bookcases, above all, books. Now, the door swung gently inwards.

The room was heavily curtained and was almost dark despite the bright morning. The light she let in showed the bookcases along the side walls. In every available space on the walls was a picture: steel engravings, small landscapes in heavy frames, and several sepia photographs of groups of boys. Like all of the rooms in the house this one widened out towards the window. On one side of the window stood a high-backed, low-seated, winged armchair; on the other was what seemed an unfeasibly small bed for such a large man as Mr Henry. The lump in the bed moved. A disordered bush of white hair appeared from under the eider-down and turned restlessly on the pillow. His face was pink, flushed and hot looking; the eyes were shut.

'Mr Henry?'

'Urgorraburb. Furt,' said her tutor. His eyelids pressed more tightly together as if he were resisting awakening.

'Are you all right?'

The answer was a tremendous sigh; the huge old face rolled on the pillow, showing only a half-smothered profile.

'Old Mr Henry not quite with us yet, then?'

Roland's voice, low and mocking, came from behind her. He came closer, staring at the man in bed. When he spoke again Julia felt his breath in her hair. It was not pleasant.

'Can't have that, eh? Old boy late on parade. Mother will have him on a fizzer. Ha.' The little laugh, only half-aspirated, was mirthless. In his dressing gown, Roland had evidently been on his way to the bathroom, a toilet bag in one hand, and a cigarette in the other. 'Shouldn't bother him,' he went on. 'He won't be up till lunchtime.'

'Breakfast is ready, Uncle,' she said very

quietly, so as not to wake Mr Henry, whose head had now almost completely disappeared beneath the eiderdown once more. 'I was told to knock on your door.'

'A delight that unfortunately I seem to have missed.' He smiled. The light from the cupola windows made his hair seem very thin, his eyes oyster-like.

'I must get back,' she said.

'Tell them the bad news, eh?'

Did he deliberately stand in her way, so that she had to squeeze past him (his arms upraised in a mock gesture of shrinking away), and brush against his chest and smell the warm rank odour under his arms?

'Tell them I'll be right down,' he called after her.

★ ★ ★

'There wasn't any chance of him getting out of it,' said Roland. 'I've looked into it thoroughly. He could have a deferment if he had already started or been accepted by a university — but he hasn't. Any other exemptions are reserved for coal miners and fishermen — trawlers and that sort of thing — the merchant marine generally, and agricultural labourers, if they are involved in essential food production — turnips etcetera

151

— the police — and their clients in prison. And who else?' He sipped at the weak, sweet coffee.

'Ah yes — lunatics, mental defectives, the blind, and clergymen. So, the boy can go mad, join the Church, put his eyes out — '

'Don't, Roland.' Evelyn shuddered.

' — go under the ground, plough the land, or put to sea. Or become a bobby.'

'I don't quite see why you are talking at such length about James avoiding the National Service,' said Mrs Covington sternly. 'The whole thing may in some respects be unfortunate or awkward, but it is his duty, together with all the other young men.'

'I agree, Ma,' said Roland. 'Why the hell should you avoid it, old son? We had to go, what with the war and all. I simply don't see the point of looking for trouble if you can possibly avoid it. But I don't see, James, that there is any way that you can avoid it.'

'I never said I wanted to avoid anything.' James looked nervously at his aunt and his grandmother. 'But I did think that I might try for the Air Force.'

'Did you tell them that at the medical?' asked Roland.

'Have you taken the medical?' asked Evelyn.

'Three weeks ago. I had an interview and a test. I think it's okay.'

'That means it'll only be another week or so before you're posted,' said Roland.

'Is that all?' said Julia, and surprised herself by how disappointed she sounded. They all stared at her.

'How will you know?' asked Mrs Covington.

'They'll send him a letter. The old brown envelope job,' said Roland.

'But surely that will go to the house in Devon or wherever?' said Mrs Covington. 'Your other grandparents?'

'I've asked them to forward it.'

'It seems you're all organised, my boy,' said Roland.

'You looked very well in uniform, Roland,' said Mrs Covington.

'After my tailor had been at it.' He glanced at his watch. 'Good God, nearly ten.'

'We're not usually this late at the breakfast table,' said Evelyn stiffly.

'What was that you said last night, Roland? About a drive?' said Mrs Covington.

'I didn't think you'd heard.' He laughed.

'I hear everything. Now — you simply must take us for a little trip out. More than that. We shall go to the sea.'

'To the sea?' said Evelyn.

'Yes. You can come too. You've looked so pale and edgy lately. All must come.'

'With my stuff in there,' said Roland, 'there's really only room for three — two with me, I mean.'

'Julia can't go,' said Evelyn. 'Her studies . . . '

'Her studies, pah,' said Mrs Covington. 'Last time I heard them they were talking about goblins or something.'

'Mermaids. And Men,' said Julia.

'Well, then, I suppose you must stay and look after your mermaids. And men,' said Mrs Covington.

'Old Henry looked a bit green about the gills this morning,' said Roland.

His mother laughed. 'There'll be no news from him today. So it is you and me, Evelyn. Come along. Come along.'

⋆ ⋆ ⋆

Julia longed for them to leave. Her grandmother had gone upstairs to dress. James had gone to his room 'to sort out things'. Roland tinkered with the car outside. Her mother said, darkly, 'Roland was always like this. You had to do what he wanted. Have you something to occupy you, Julia?'

No, she had nothing. Her mother knew

this. But, yes, she said, she had some work to do for Mr Henry. Her mother nodded in satisfaction. Thus they maintained the fiction between them.

'He should be up, surely, before long,' said her mother. 'I really have never known him to lie in bed like this before.'

'It will give me a chance to catch up on my homework,' said Julia. How ridiculous, she thought — it is all homework.

'Yes. Good.' Her mother looked at her for what seemed a very long time. Then she said, 'We really must have a proper talk soon, Julia. I sometimes forget you are growing up. It is very difficult for me — to see that.'

For one moment Julia thought that her mother was going to embrace her. She knew that if that happened she would surely cry and clutch on to her. But her mother only blinked and moved her mouth in an odd way, then said, 'I must go. We will talk. This absurd outing . . . ' The moment had been safely negotiated; once more they had avoided intimacy. This woman, Julia reminded herself, was her mother. Surely, she must love her mother? Why then did she regard her for much of the time as a tiresome harridan, as a woman whose face had become riddled over the past few years with a horrid, pouchy-cheeked, tight-lipped look of self-pity, whose eyes looked blank and unseeing behind the spectacles she now wore all the time. It seemed that all sense of humour, of life, and of love had withered inside this woman. Worse, it was as if she wanted these things to wither in Julia too, almost before they had had chance to take root.

'Well, are we ready?' Mrs Covington came into the hall. If she had not carried herself with such an unshakeable sense of her own importance, Julia thought that her grand-mother might have looked slightly ridiculous. Even so, she did look rather odd. Her driving clothes came from the twenties. The long brown leather coat dropped almost to her ankles. The black cloche hat sported a long, iridescent peacock feather at one side.

'It is astonishing,' she said. 'I have not worn these things for almost twenty years and they still fit me perfectly.'

'Grandmama,' said Julia, laughing, 'you look absolutely terrific.'

'Oh God,' said Evelyn faintly.

'Do you think so, my dear. That's very kind.' Mrs Covington smiled at herself in the hall mirror. Her teeth were yellow with one brown tooth like a gate in a fence.

'Are you sure this is a good idea, Mother? The weather is clouding over again. Up on the coast it will probably pour down.'

156

'Goodness — you are so hopeless, Evelyn. When my generation were made in the last century they used sterner stuff than of late. We shall go. You have had a holiday this year — I have been absolutely nowhere.'

It was true — the sky was clouding over, but Mrs Covington was determined.

The party set off for the sea.

⋆ ⋆ ⋆

When she came back into the hall after waving them off, Julia experienced a strange sensation. On the rare occasions when she had been left alone before the house had seemed larger, now it felt somehow smaller and somehow constricting. And she knew it was because of the presence of a newcomer in the house — young, male, unseen, but very definitely felt. She wanted to see James. What was he doing upstairs? Perhaps she could walk out in the garden, circle the house and pass under his window. He would look down and she would pretend to be surprised. And what then? She would ask him down, to go for a walk with her. To the village — that would be a pleasant transgression against her mother's absurd laws. Only yesterday evening, James had suggested that Julia show him around the village. Her mother had said

157

coldly, 'I do not particularly care for Julia to go out at this time of night.'

Now they were on their own — apart from the sleeping form of Mr Henry. How many hours, days, weeks, months, God — years, had she spent doing absolutely nothing. The thought was terrifying. It couldn't be that her life was normal. Years ago, had she gone to school and been with other children. Those children had stayed on at school. They had formed friendships and had adventures, perhaps ones as good as those she read about in books; the ones that girls had with girls, and boys with boys. And, then, all that other world, of Shakespeare and poets and the novelists, where girls and boys became young men and women. And fell — what was that? — in love. What was that? She considered James. She looked at herself in the long hall mirror, which showed a slightly darkened image of the garden through the open double doors. What was there visible in her face that corresponded to his? They were first cousins, after all. But their parents — brother and sister — were so wildly different. Her view of Roland fluctuated between thinking him lively and funny, and being — what? Surely he couldn't think of her in that way? But he had made her slide past him this morning, and then there was the way that he looked at her sometimes. And the families they had had — she and James were both the only children of each marriage. That was an odd coincidence. And they were both an inch taller than their parents. They both had the same brown hair, though his looked fairer being cut quite short. The hairs on his tanned arms were a dark gold. Why did she think of his arms? They were both tall and slim and — give or take a bit here and there, she laid her hands on her breasts and smiled at the thought — they might be twins, or reflections in this mirror. It was not possible, was it? To feel anything for a first cousin? There was the blood connection. But first cousins . . . She stared at her face, she ran her fingers down each side and knew that she was searching for the eyes and the cheekbones and the lines of the mouth of James.

What else was there to do in this house but search the mirrors? Even if you did not look in them directly, they showed you moving from one room to another, those mirrored rooms somehow stiller and paler; and there was no air in those other rooms, the light was borrowed, the reflected people actors, their faces and bodies slightly distorted and very faintly discoloured, like the recently dead.

Look on. Look on. You spent years in the mirror, yet it held no time at all. It mimicked the depth of the room, but had a hard, cold, impenetrable surface. You were reversed in the mirror and thought that you were still real, but the titles of the books behind you were in a new, unknown language and there was a strange green tint in the far high cornices of the mirrored room.

She looked on. And that green colour seeped into the hall and into her skin. The longer you looked the more you belonged in that other room.

She heard the door at the bottom of the stairs open behind her, and James stood in the mirror.

★ ★ ★

They sat, one at each end of the long chintz-covered sofa in the room they called the library. The sun was shining at that moment through fast-moving rain clouds and Julia had opened the windows to the garden.

'The grass is still wet, I'm afraid. Otherwise we might sit on it,' she said.

James smiled a little too broadly.

'What are you laughing at?'

'I'm sorry. It's nothing. It's very nice. It's just the terribly formal way you speak. Like a book. A very good book, of course.'

'What do you mean — a book?' Her voice

was sharper and she felt sorry for that and knew that she sounded like her mother, her voice in search of an argument, or an imagined slight.

'It's simply — your life here is very different, isn't it? Old Mr Henry teaching you all on your own — that's what Dad said he was doing. It's not very often you find that.'

'Mr Henry's very sweet. He knows absolutely everything and he's read everything.'

'He taught Dad.' James stopped, then went on hesitantly. 'Dad said that he used to read them the most extraordinary things. He was a bit sort of — well — pansified. They used to rag him an awful lot. You know what boys are like.'

'No, I don't. I don't think you should talk about Mr Henry like that.'

They stared at each other. James cleared his throat, looked over his shoulder at the bookshelves, then out into the garden.

'What is there to do here?'

'To do?' She laughed. 'Not much, I'm afraid. I don't know what would interest you. There's the village.'

'What's there?'

'A school. A church. A pub.'

'That'll do for Dad. I might take a walk down there. Would you come down with me?'

This time, their eyes met. 'You could show me round.'

'I don't know if I can do that. My mother doesn't like me going to the village without her.'

'You'd be with me. There'd be no harm.'

'No, I can't. Not without her permission. We don't do things that way.'

'Ok-ay.' He drew the second syllable out. 'If we have to stay in.'

'*We* don't have to stay in, James. You can perfectly well go to the village on your own if you want.' Again, she was aware that she had misjudged the tone of her voice. She sounded prim where she had meant to sound teasing. The poor boy must think her mad. Or, worse, that she was dull and silly.

'No, no. I don't want to leave you all on your own.' He spoke in an earnest, rather sweet way.

'I'm not alone. Mr Henry's here.'

'In bed. Not well. Not at all well, according to Dad.'

'Was he drunk last night?'

'Didn't you see?'

'I thought he was a bit giggly and silly. He can be like that sometimes anyway.'

'Dad told me that Mr Henry used to entertain what he called his Prometheans. He chose them from the boys he thought were the most talented. They used to drink sherry in his rooms.'

'Are you talented?' she said shyly. She wanted to reward him because she had been sharp with him.

'Me? No. I play the piano a bit.'

'Really? How wonderful. What do you play?'

'The usual stuff. The sort you always learn as a kid. Bits of Beethoven and Schubert and Mozart — all the easy bits. And some jazz.'

'I don't know anything about jazz.'

'Haven't you got a wireless or a record player?'

'There's Mr Henry's gramophone in the corner.' She pointed.

'Does it play LPs?'

'Yes. Mr Henry has some. I don't know if you'd like them.'

'That's terrific. And you've got a piano?'

'In the sitting room. It's always locked though.'

'Doesn't matter. I've brought some records with me. We can have some music.'

He jumped up. 'Wait here,' he said.

When he rushed back a couple of minutes later his face was radiant with excitement, his eyes bright. He stood in front of her and said, 'Wait till you hear this.'

6

'Not the most unwasted of days.' Evelyn spoke with an attempt at heavy irony.

'For heaven's sake, Evelyn,' said Mrs Covington. 'What else would you have been doing at this time? Apart from drinking your filthy herbal tea and reading Agatha Christie.'

'Agatha Christie is preferable to Warwick Deeping,' said Evelyn.

What did the man say, thought Roland — that there is no disputing between a louse and a flea?

The vertiginously angled mountain passes had been left behind. The Malverns declined in the south, and the flat Midlands plain opened before him. The sky was a mass of rain cloud with just a few tiny patches of washed-out blue. The rain had stopped, but showers had accompanied them most of the day. And for the greater part of the day Roland had had to listen to his mother and sister bickering in the car.

No, it had not been a good day and it was not made better by being reminded of that fact by Evelyn every five minutes. They had decided to motor to Bangor. It was the nearest place to the sea that was not awfully vulgar, according to Mrs Covington. Besides, her late husband, Roland's dear father, had an unmarried female cousin of some order in Beaumaris — although it would not be necessary to visit her.

For a while, on the way up the A5, Roland had kept up a facetious commentary on what could be seen out of the windows. To their left, a glacial valley of gigantic pebbles; to their right, a decayed Welsh village; to their left again, a decayed Welsh peasant; up ahead, a number of sheep, looking like maggots from down here . . .

'Don't be disgusting, Roland,' Evelyn snapped.

The rain had seemed only a fine mist, but in the mountains the water ran off the rocks like thick twisting black snakes. In Bangor, rain swept in from the sea and drove horizontally across the pier.

'Welshman's weather,' said Roland.

'The people cannot be held responsible,' said Evelyn.

'No, just look at them.'

They would, Mrs Covington announced, go over to Anglesey. They would lunch at the hotel in Beaumaris.

As the car had gone over the bridge,

Roland reflected on how wonderful it would be if they — if he — could just keep on driving, driving, until you came to America. Driving through the grey waves and under the brilliant unwavering stars until you arrived at a new life. Freedom. Solvency. He would have no regrets at leaving — especially not these two women.

His mother was repeating to Evelyn the names of the birds and flowers and trees she saw as they went through the narrow lanes. Yellow wagtail. Chaffinch. Wild orchid. Sooty fern. Another fern.

'One good fern deserves another,' said Roland.

'Do shut up, Roland,' said Evelyn.

'Yes, do,' said his mother. 'That tree — there — in that person's garden. Extraordinary. How did that get there?'

Yes, he could certainly do without these two. And the boy was of an age to start looking after himself. Margaret had flown the coop. He hadn't got what you might call a lot of friends. He had never gone in much for friends.

'This is Beaumaris,' his mother announced. 'Go into the town. The hotel is on the right at the end of the High Street.'

That's what he must do, Roland thought, as the sun slanted in from America. *Get*

Away, Get Away, Get Away, the wiper blade whispered on the windscreen.

★ ★ ★

Mr Henry woke again. His hair was damp and his mouth was parched. The pure, red-hot pain of the morning had abated, but still, above his right eye squatted a demon, gently and endlessly twisting some awl-like implement into his forehead. He was grateful to wake. He had been dreaming intensely. In his dream he had been in a great abandoned and wrecked city. Every door hung off one hinge; the streets were full of broken glass, oil-slicked gutters, splintered roof beams, broken bricks. He was searching, searching quite ignobly for a lavatory. He found an archway with steps leading into the earth and into an utterly befouled and puddled public convenience. It was so disgusting that he could not possibly use it. Then came the music. It crept insidiously through the walls, down through the broken frosted-glass roof. An awful music that thumped and yelled at him, mocking his delicacy and his revulsion at this filthy place. He could not use it. He could not use any of these beshitted stalls, with their broken lavatory bowls and seats,

167

their smashed, dried cisterns. The unspeak-able — what was it? He couldn't. Couldn't . . .

Now that he was awake he became aware of the uncomfortable pressure of his bladder. Why did he dream of ordure, of horrors? He didn't deserve *those*. He had been dreaming — but now the music returned. Real, it seeped treacherously through the floor from the library below. A distant booming, a bass being plucked. Only that. Then he heard a trumpet barking in a ludicrous series of sounds. He must see what on earth it was. But the most serious thing must be attended to at once. He rose painfully and padded to the door. He put on his dressing gown over his pyjamas. Never normally would he proceed through the house in such a state of undress, but his need drove him. On the gallery landing the noise was much louder. It *was* coming from the library. Absurd. No such sound had ever been heard in this house before. Going to the balustrade, he peered over. The musical racket stopped abruptly. He thought he heard Julia's voice. Where was everyone else? Why had Mrs Walters not run across the hall to quell the noise? He tried to remember what had happened on the previous night; it came to him that Roland had given everyone far too much wine, and had then insisted on finishing off with whisky.

Dust hung in a shaft of sunlight striking into the well. It was — he twisted to see the clock down in the hall — it was four-thirty on an August afternoon, and he was standing disgracefully enough in his night attire. This was the first non-holiday weekday on which he had missed going down to the village for the newspaper. The first such day that he had not prepared his report. It was quite unforgivable. God knows, his duties were few and light enough. The education of Julia was regarded as complete, at least by Mrs Covington, he knew. If he failed to serve any purpose in the household, what was to become of him?

He must get dressed and shaved and then go straight down and find out what on earth Julia meant by that filthy sound. It was the coming of the men to the house, the coming of Roland, that was to blame. Paradise had been disturbed — a poor enough paradise, but the only one he had.

★ ★ ★

'He reads the news to you all every day?'

'Not just reads — he prepares what he calls a 'bulletin'. He recites, no, he retails it over lunch every day. I sometimes think he makes

169

it up. Or, at least, changes the bad news a little this way or that to please my grandmother.'

'Don't you have a wireless at all? Why don't you all just listen to the news on that?'

'I think Mr Henry has one in his room. I'm not supposed to listen to it.'

'Did you like that?' James pointed to the gramophone.

'I'd never heard anything like it before. It's fine.'

That was not sufficient praise. He had just played her his favourite record, the one that annoyed his grandfather so: *Singin' the Blues*. Every time he heard the cornet solo, it was like walking on an island that no one else had ever walked on. The island's air had never been breathed before and its single bird on its one tree had sung unheard for ever. But it was a place of solitude and he had never before shared it with anyone, in case they should misunderstand. Quite a few boys at school listened to jazz, mostly New Orleans or white Chicago style. There was a club that met each Saturday evening in one of the classrooms to play and discuss records. But, to James, to pool their pleasure was to dilute that pleasure. None of the others — he was sure of this — none of them brought to their listening the same votive passion as he did.

170

The Bix record was not just 'jazz', it was his youth; although made thirty years ago, it contained youth as an immortal current running through successive generations. And he had played it to Julia because she was young and he thought that she would feel the same rapt, warm sensual pathway opening in her mind. Of course, to do so was a sort of betrayal of himself. He had played the record for her, and all she could find to say was that it was 'fine'.

He turned the disc over, his back to her. The music began to beat out. *Muskrat Ramble*.

He faced her; her eyes were full of light from the garden, which had suddenly brightened.

'Oh, I like that better. It's jolly. Jollier,' she said.

Yes it was. Jolly. Jollier.

'Would you like to dance?' he heard himself say.

'What kind of dance can you do to this?' But she stood up and held out her arms at shoulder height.

'No,' he said. 'Like this.' He took her left hand and said, 'Now you twist around. Twirl around. While I sort of move about.'

They danced slowly and awkwardly at first, but then moved more smoothly and less self-consciously on to the carpet in the middle of the room.

Her face was remarkably composed in a new studied happiness as she watched his feet and every now and then swept her hair back and stared into his face.

'What do you call this?' she shouted above the music.

'*Muskrat Ramble* — it's by the same band.'

'No — the dance. What's the dance called?'

'Jiving.'

Julia's cool fingers slid in and almost out of his hand and her body twisted half this way, half that. Her narrow waist swivelled on her hips.

The record ended.

'I'll take it off.' There was a thickness in his throat, a lump that his words had to get around. He felt awkward as he walked to the gramophone, knowing she was watching him; that she stood there, expectantly — in the way girls seemed to have of waiting for you to act. 'If you don't take them off straight away the needle knocks in the groove and wears out.'

'Have you any others?'

'Upstairs. Is there anything among these?'

'They're Mr Henry's. Not to be played. And the old 78s are my great-uncle Edgar's. They've been there for years. Nobody's touched them in all that time except me and I've given up playing them. I got bored. A lot are terrible, but Grandmother says that we're too poor to throw anything away.'

'My father says that Grandma's quite rich. Sorry. I mean with the farms and this house and everything.'

'I don't know about that.' She sat down on the sofa again. 'There certainly never seems to be money to spare.'

'Shall I put this on again?' He held the record up.

'No. It will spoil it. Repeating the same thing too soon spoils the first time, don't you think? Sit down here and tell me about this awful Army call-up.'

'The Air Force. I told you I did my medical and all. It's practically decided. A week or so and I'm in it.'

'That's not fair.'

'What do you mean?'

'It doesn't give you much time, does it? I mean, you've only just left school.'

He had been expecting perhaps a different sort of answer; instead she had made him feel like a schoolboy.

They sat in silence for a few moments, then she said, 'When do you go?'

'As soon as — '

'I heard a noise. A most dreadful noise.' Mr

Henry stood in the doorway. He did not look well; his face was flushed and his white hair stood on end as if electrified.

They both looked at him.

'What sort of a noise?' said Julia.

'Quite dreadful. Dance music of some sort.' His head twisted slowly inside his collar, like an ancient turtle's moving in its shell. 'You have been playing records.'

'Yes,' said Julia, smiling at him. 'We have.'

'Well, certainly not my records, thank goodness,' said Mr Henry. 'It sounded like the sort of thing I used to catch the boys playing many years ago. *Jazz* music.'

'I'm afraid they still do play them, Mr Henry,' said James.

'Yes, we used to call it *Jazz music*.'

Oh God, thought James, let the man shut up and go away. He had spoiled everything. What was it about the old that so infuriated him? He answered himself — their wilful and continued and implacable ignorance and hatred of anything that made the young happy and life worthwhile.

'I suppose if you must — if you wish to play it. But it is so infernally clangorous.'

'We shan't play any more,' said Julia gravely. Mr Henry wondered if she was making fun of him.

'How are you feeling now, Mr Henry?'

James forced himself to ask.

'Feeling? I think I must have contracted a rather bad cold. I can only apologise, Julia, that you have missed a day of learning.'

'Well, no harm done, Mr Henry. And I think it is the holiday period. I know that this is not school as such, but Mother did say until the end of July. And today is the second of August.'

'Ah — so yesterday was a supererogatory day too. But I must say, Julia, that I hardly think that Mrs Walters would quite approve of this . . . ' He waved a hand dismissively at the gramophone. 'By the way, where are your mother and grandmother?'

'They've gone to the seaside, Mr Henry,' she said in that mock grave voice again. Was she trying to humour, to tease him? To show him up as a foolish old man? It must be the presence of this young man. That must be it. She had never spoken to him like this before.

'I hope the weather has been kinder to them than it has been here,' he said.

★ ★ ★

It was late evening before the party got home.

'I hope,' said Mrs Covington, 'that Julia has had the sense to prepare some sort of supper for us.'

There was no telephone at the Round House, so it had been impossible to signal their time of arrival. Roland had facetiously suggested sending a telegram and Mrs Covington had seriously considered the idea, then decided against it because of the expense involved. 'We can rely on the girl's good sense,' she said.

As they could. Julia had prepared a cold supper of sausage and cheese, eggs and salad. James, she explained, had gone out for a walk.

After supper, Mr Henry excused himself and followed Evelyn into the kitchen, shutting the door behind him. He came out a few minutes later and announced that he was retiring to bed.

'I wonder what the old boy's up to with Evelyn. Most mysterious.' Roland chuckled, and headed off to the cellar for a bottle of wine.

'Well, let's hope he's well tomorrow,' said Mrs Covington. 'Then we can get back to normal.'

'Did you have a good time?' Julia asked.

'A splendid day,' said her grandmother. 'Though not all would agree. But I, at least, enjoyed myself. It's all in the state of mind.'

7

Mr Henry was up at seven o'clock the following morning. It was Mrs Fellowes' day off, she would not be coming up from the village to clean and he was glad. He put on an apron and proceeded to wash up the dishes left from last night's supper. A bonus, if of a somewhat humiliating kind, was when Evelyn came into the kitchen at just before eight. He had been working very slowly, hoping for just such a visit, keeping a couple of plates back, dawdling over them as the water in the basin grew increasingly lukewarm, gazing out to the battlements of the square church tower above the high garden hedge.

'Good morning, Mr Henry. Busy early. Couldn't you sleep?'

There was no humour, and only a trace of goodwill in her voice. Yet he was pathetically grateful for her attention. He was showing he was of use in some way, however demeaning it might be.

She put the kettle on the hob and wandered out of the kitchen. When the kettle eventually whistled, she reappeared and made a pot of tea, slowly and silently. She poured herself a cup, did not offer him one, and went out again, carrying her cup and saucer. There was never a formal breakfast on the charlady's day off. Evelyn would have returned to her room, not be seen again until lunchtime. He poured himself tea. He sat down at the kitchen table and pondered the terrors of life.

It really was appalling, the way time simply disappeared. Worse was the feeling that the past was somehow still *there*, somewhere, all still there, as real and living as . . . not *now* — obviously not . . . but the past was living, and growing monstrously as they fed it, literally, each of their finished days. What, for instance, had happened to his plan to translate the *Georgics* this summer? He had tried, here and there, but his Latin had slipped disastrously. He had wanted to trounce Day-Lewis, who had converted his beloved Virgil's poetry into long, loose, sloppy lines full of all sorts of inaccuracy and anachronism. Mr Henry had, after three weeks, only managed to translate half a page, and that not to his satisfaction. The very idea of translating poetry was nonsense anyway. What English could render *sed fugit interea, fugit irreparabile tempus*? Time, that cannot be restored . . . ? Perhaps some of Tennyson came close to the concentration of sweet sounds:

The moan of doves in immemorial elms,
And murmuring of innumerable bees.

But there was none of the Italian light, the pagan element — Tennyson was good, but too English in the end, too whiskery. Ah, how Mr Henry wished he had someone to tell such things to.

At ten he put on his summer blazer and went to the village to collect *The Times*. He must put on a bravura performance today to counteract the impression his enforced idleness must have given yesterday.

★　★　★

Roland woke at about eight, turned over, and went back to sleep for another hour. He was in that delicious warm state where sleep can be summoned at will and when dreams become an almost controllable reverie. He dreamed the most odd things. There were three boys on one bike, a boy astride the crossbar, a boy on the saddle, pedalling, and a boy standing on the case carrier above the back wheel, holding with one hand on to the shoulder of the pedaller, and raising the other

179

hand in triumph as they sped down a long, long, inclined suburban road. The boy on the back of the bike was himself, Roland. At the same time he was watching the boy from between bedroom curtains and he was the boy speeding and whooping down the road. This was amusing, but, drifting near to waking, he wanted more from his dream. He called for girls he had known years before. Their faces, though, eluded him, melting and re-forming into Margaret's face or, more alarmingly in one instance, into that of his grandmother. Their bodies too refused quite to conform. He wished to undress them slowly; they immediately became naked. He reinstated their clothes; they began to talk to one another, ignoring him, as if he were some silent film director who had lost his authority, pacing just out of camera, barking unheeded instructions through a megaphone. Silent, indeed. He shifted in the bed, from discomfort back to comfort. He thought of a woman he had met a few years back in London. What was her name? Janine, that was it. His half-dream attempted to half-undress her. He reached down to fondle himself. He drew his hand back after a minute. He really was too old for that game. It killed your desire. Forty-four years old now — he had another ten good years at most. Then that was it. Flatteau had told him that in a pub once. 'Fifty, old boy — forget it. Not only don't the women look at you any more — they don't even *see* you any more.'

He rolled on to his back. His eyes were open fully now. He stared at the ceiling. It was bowed and yellowed with damp, a crack ran in the plaster from one corner to another, joined here and there by tributary fractures. The bloody place was falling down. But it still must be worth a bob or two. The farms as well. And the land. Pity it was miles from anywhere. They could build an airport here. The *Roland Covington Lounge*, serving light meals, refreshments and alcoholic beverages. He would plough in all the hedges and the trees and twee little cottages and the grey church that looked like a giant snail in the rain. Bugger it all — he hated the lot. Well, it wasn't his, was it? Not likely to be for a while. He could hardly live his life out waiting for his mother to die. And when she did hand in her lunch pail, there was the question of having to share everything with Evelyn. He lay and his mind rambled through pastures of pure idleness available after the funeral. Of being the lord of the manor here; striding across the hall in noisy brand-new expensive riding boots; or riding on a chestnut mare, high above the locals touching their forelocks and tipping their caps to him. However and meanwhile, there was the small consideration of how to make ends meet right now. He could stop here for some time, no doubt. The old girl was favourably disposed at the moment. Evelyn was a pain in the arse, as always. And it was a good time to be out of London. That hundred he owed Sandy Ferrers — God knows, Sandy had enough, but he wouldn't let that go. He dragged the sheet over his shoulder. It had all been so simple years ago; school and his parents, then the war to take care of him, and Margaret, and the others — why did it all have to get so bloody complicated the older you got? Sometimes, if he let it, the whole prospect terrified him — to find himself at his age with no job, no career, no bloody money. Well, something had to be done, old chap, no doubt about that. But no hurry. No hurry today. Sleep a bit more. Get up, shave. Breakfast. Go and have a drink in the Dog. Few years more.

Roland curled himself into a foetal ball and slept; this time the dreamless sleep of the guiltless.

★ ★ ★

Evelyn was concerned. Last night, after supper, Mr Henry had wondered if he might possibly 'have a word'. She was sitting in the kitchen, listening to Roland's voice behind the closed service hatch. Roland had been drinking throughout the meal — Mother simply encouraged him by listening and cooing and laughing and arguing and, oh, just encouraging him to behave badly. He had always been the one, hadn't he? The darling boy. They were all darling boys — until they became men. So, what was this that Mr Henry was trying to tell her? James? And Julia? Music in the afternoon. Jig-a-boo music. What on earth was he talking about? Loud, clattering music of the type — he believed — they called jazz. And she had said, 'Come on, Mr Henry, you are not quite that ancient.'

'Well, I know the sound, Mrs Walters, and I must admit that it jars upon me. Besides, it was played so very loudly. And when I went down — when I went into the library to see . . . '

'Well, what did you see?'

'Um, nothing, Nothing as such, that is to say. But I could swear that Julia and James had been dancing. I could tell by their colour — and by a certain air of what, what I can describe as a sort of exaltation, a spirit of rampancy . . . '

'Are you going mad, Mr Henry? I have, quite frankly, never heard anyone use such absurd language. Have you been drinking?'

Roland's voice droned on in the next room.

'I thought it my duty to bring it to your attention,' Mr Henry said stiffly. 'You have placed me — for part of the time, at least — in loco parentis to the girl.'

'The 'girl' is my daughter, Mr Henry. Remember that.'

Red-faced, mumbling, making an apologetic withdrawal, Mr Henry had gone to bed.

But Julia and James were cousins, first cousins. It could only be a light flirtation. Perhaps there would come a day when Julia was attracted to a man; certainly a day when she was pursued by one. When the world finally possessed her. And all of that world seemed to be collapsing, degenerating into a mass of rebellion, insolence and immorality. The very order of their lives, which had held for centuries, was threatened. They must hold on for as long as they could. They must last a little longer for Julia's sake. For the sake of the family.

Evelyn was proud of the fact that her own mother could trace her forebears back almost two hundred years, the details written in various dead hands in the front of the family bible. Her father's side dwindled into the fog of nondescript history in the middle of the nineteenth century. And her husband's family had no history at all: foot soldiers and labourers, a rumoured publican here, a half-remembered groom there. But the Covingtons had *risen*, hadn't they? From their admittedly lowly origins they had established themselves in the comfortable, the respected — and respectable — English middle class, the backbone of the professions; the Land; the Bank . . . And all the modern poisons had been kept from Julia. Julia would run as clean and clear as a stream. First cousins. There was no law against first cousins. What? Against first cousins doing what? Evelyn's mind became a blank. There was nothing that these young people could do, was there? Nothing in that way. What way? It was absurd. No, any emotional give and take between them would be based purely on family sentiment, on friendship and consanguinity. There was no question of . . . Of any emotional, of any — and she barely thought the word into the barest of existences — any *sexual* interest between them. The sexual component of her own life was now so far in the past that she was able almost to regard her own daughter as the product of some virginal parthenogenesis.

185

Not that, she shuddered, there was anything Catholic or Papist about her distaste. Perhaps it had been love, in the beginning, with Rex. He had let her down in the end. It was in the nature of the animal. Rex — the name of a dog. So, they would have to keep the young people apart. Fortunately, James would be going into the Air Force soon. Was it wicked of her to think like that? With this awful trouble in Egypt, it looked as if our boys would be needed again, and soon. Well, they must do their duty, as her generation had. Until then the boy must be found something to occupy him.

Now, lunch. What was there for their lunch?

★　★　★

'Mr Henry,' said Mrs Covington, 'it seems a long time since we have heard from you.'

'Hear, hear.'

'Be quiet, Roland — you don't know what I am talking about. I hope you are quite recovered, Mr Henry, from your mysterious upset. You are well again?'

'Yes. Thank you, Mrs Covington.' Mr Henry smiled bravely at the other faces round the table.

'The form is, my dear Roland and James.'

Mrs Covington inclined her grey head to the newcomers. 'The form is that we have our very own news service, in the shape of our good friend here.'

The good friend was suitably modest.

'You should know, Roland — if I may — I know I taught you as a boy, but I can hardly now call you 'Covington' at your own, um, table — and James — equally, if I may — you should know that it has never been my intention to dominate the luncheon table with my own asseverations — '

'Get on with it,' said Mrs Covington.

'Yes. Of course. It started — '

'It started with Mr Henry reading *The Times* to us,' said Evelyn.

'Not quite all of it — '

'That became extremely tedious,' said Evelyn.

'In short,' said Mrs Covington, 'it was decided that we should ask Mr Henry to make up a sort of daily . . . What would you call it, Mr Henry? A sort of composite?'

'More of a *compote* perhaps,' Mr Henry said, snuffling with delight at his own wit.

'Yes. A sort of composite rendition. And he has done it very well. Though I think that sometimes, out of deference to our more delicate feelings, he has not told us the whole truth.'

'I can't wait,' said Roland. 'But I must warn you, Mr Henry, that I shall go down to the village later and check every word.'

'You can't do that,' said Evelyn. 'It would spoil the whole thing.'

Roland silently mouthed 'the whole thing' back at his sister, in the way he had done as a child, to annoy her.

'Now, now, settle down,' said Mrs Covington. 'Begin, Mr Henry. Begin.'

'The crisis of which I spoke earlier this week, the illegal seizure of the Suez Canal, yesterday resulted in a debate in Parliament, in both Houses, of Lords and Commons. That, we may say, was the headline news. Before, however, I proceed to the gist of the debate, I would like, as is my custom, to preface my larger report with some smaller items of news of a somewhat more diverting nature.'

'Thank God for that,' said Roland in a low voice.

Evelyn hissed sharply.

'As always — the weather first. A high pressure area continues in the North Atlantic and I fear that the present blustery and rainy conditions are likely to hold over the weekend.'

'It is August Bank Holiday weekend — what else do you expect?'

188

'Roland, please don't be tiresome,' said Mrs Covington, intervening before Evelyn could protest more violently.

'Though the temperature should rise a little, perhaps as high as the mid-sixties.' He paused for a moment to shuffle his notes.

'Other items. The last veteran of the Union Army in the American Civil War, one Albert Woolson, has passed away at the age of one hundred and nine. He joined the Grand Army of the Republic in 1864 as a drummer boy, aged seventeen. He was, *The Times* remarks, 'a remarkably robust character. Even after he passed his century he continued to smoke eight cigars a day.''

'Bravo for Albert,' said Roland. 'Sorry.' He reached into his pocket and brought out a packet of cigarettes.

'We do not normally smoke at lunchtime,' said Evelyn.

'Pooh — that's all right, Evelyn,' said Mrs Covington, waving a hand to dismiss the protest forming on Evelyn's lips. 'It is nice to have a man smoke after all these years.'

Roland lit up, watched by them all in silence. He tilted his head back and blew out a slow blue-grey column of smoke.

'May I continue?' said Mr Henry. 'So — also — Shanghai has been struck by a typhoon. No Europeans are reported injured.

In the Seychelles Islands, there have been complaints about the behaviour of the Chief Justice. The matter was raised yesterday in the Commons. The main allegations, by a Labour member, being that 'the public and frequent drunkenness of Mr Lyon in this small place is now a by-word and a scandal . . . ''

'I don't think we want to know that.' Evelyn shifted irritably in her seat. 'It's mere tittle-tattle.'

'Precisely, my dear Mrs Walters, what the Minister said in reply. He said that the Chief Justice — being a servant of the Crown — was obviously not in a position to defend himself.'

'Then why read it out?'

'Now, Evelyn,' said Mrs Covington. 'Mr Henry, may we come to the real matter, the main meat of your bulletin — the affair in the Suez Canal?'

'Certainly,' said Mr Henry briskly. 'As I was, regrettably, unable to report yester-day — '

'We were out anyway,' said Evelyn.

' — the debate in Parliament yesterday was prefaced by a series of questions on the day before, on Wednesday. Questions, if I may say, of varying degrees of impertinence, laid by Labour members. One actually asked if the

190

Foreign Secretary had sought the assistance of the Soviet government!'

'Preposterous. Who is the Foreign Secretary?' said Mrs Covington.

'Mr Selwyn Lloyd.'

'Ah.'

'But it was the Prime Minister himself who led the debate.'

'Sir Anthony?'

'Sir Anthony.'

'What wonderful innocence the name conjures up,' said Roland.

Mr Henry, sure in his knowledge of protection by the ladies, gabbled on, quoting from the Prime Minister's words.

''Anger and alarm . . . this great international waterway . . . Colonel Nasser's past record . . . physical interference . . . how possible for us to believe the Egyptians' words?''

'What word would *they* have to give?' said Mrs Covington.

'' . . . ceaseless barrage of propaganda . . . intrigue and subversion in our territories . . . arbitrary action in breach of solemn undertakings . . . impossible to compensate . . . the nature of the regime with which we have to deal . . . violation . . . certain precautionary measures of a military nature . . . reserves recalled . . . freedom and security

. . . political repercussions throughout the Middle East . . . the world . . . an Arab Empire from the Atlantic to the Persian Gulf . . . threat . . . aggression'.'

'Good. Perhaps we shall get somewhere now,' said Mrs Covington.

'And what of little Mr Gaitskell?' asked Evelyn. 'The leader of our so-called loyal opposition?'

'The usual mixture, I am afraid, Mrs Walters, of a little sense with much absurdity. He began well, by comparing Colonel Nasser to Mussolini and Hitler, then prayed in aid of the United Nations and said that, while the use of force could not be ruled out, we must be sure that circumstances justify it.'

'Pshaw. Scuttle. Scuttle. Scuttle,' said Mrs Covington.

'But,' Mr Henry said triumphantly, 'I am proud to report that the Government is making preparations. Bomber planes are being sent to Malta. Aircraft carriers are on the move. The Privy Council is to meet this very day — perhaps at this very moment — and Her Majesty the Queen will issue the proclamation to call up reservists.'

'No, no, I think you're wrong there, Mr Henry.' Roland consulted his watch. 'I think you'll find they're probably all out at lunch just now.'

'This is not a joke, Roland,' said Evelyn. 'We know how you must make fun of everything, but we are talking of grave matters here.'

'Oh God,' he said, 'if I never made a joke about anything else, this would be one of the funniest.'

'What do you mean?'

'What do *you* mean? Sitting here, in the green, damp, comfortable heart of England, gaily declaring war on a fly-ridden dust-bowl halfway around the world — about which, by the way, you know absolutely nothing.'

'I — nothing? Unlike you, dear brother, I happen to have travelled through the Canal, as have Mother and Julia.'

'It meant nothing to you, now or then, though, did it? A rather unpleasant smelly place full of fuzzy-wuzzies — just another part of our glorious empire.'

'I happen to think the Empire is rather glorious, Roland.'

'Was. Was. The Glory that was Greece, the Splendour that was Rome, and all that. It's all gone, or going. There isn't any empire. There isn't anything out there any more. You're fighting with ghosts, Evelyn.'

'And see what a mess they're making of it, in the places where we have pulled out. As soon as we left India they began to slaughter one another.'

'They did that before we left,' said Mrs Covington. 'I saw the aftermath of the riots in Calcutta towards the end of the war. Don't forget that. They proved then that they were certainly not capable of running the country as we had done.'

'We didn't manage it — we conquered and occupied it.'

'Don't be absurd, Roland,' said Mrs Covington evenly. 'We held India with a comparative handful of men. A handful, compared to the millions and millions of *them*.'

'Men like Father, I suppose? We're all very grand. Old India hands and all that. Well, Dad was a bank manager. In England, that's what he was, and good luck to him. Send him out to India though, and he becomes a great man. Then an object deserving of pity because the natives want the place back and he has to leave.'

'You go too far, Roland,' said Mrs Covington. 'Your father was a good servant to India, to his King and Country.'

'I hope you can say the same, Roland,' said Evelyn.

'I fought for King and Country, dear Evelyn, while you sat out the war in India, if I remember correctly. Or what you imagined was India.'

'What do you mean — imagined?'

'Well — the jolly old Club. And the servants. From the way you talk about it, it was as if the country, *India*, was never there. What you had was a kind of hot Surbiton really, wasn't it?'

Mrs Covington's chair scraped on the floor as she rose from the table.

'Oh dear. Dear, dear,' she said. 'I think that's quite enough for one day. If you knew what you were talking about, Roland, I might find such a discussion interesting. Dinner will be at seven. I look forward to seeing you then in a perhaps slightly better frame of mind.'

When she had gone out, shepherded by Evelyn, Roland sat back and lit another cigarette.

'Put up a bit of a black, it seems, boys and girls, eh?'

James looked steadfastly down at his empty plate. Julia gazed at Mr Henry's hands as he shuffled together the small sheets of yellow paper he used for his notes.

'Well, say something,' said Roland. 'Somebody.'

'I found, if I may say so, Roland,' said Mr Henry, 'your remarks very ill-advised.'

8

Roland did not appear for dinner that evening. He had left a note for Mrs Covington on the rent table. He wrote that he was sorry if he had upset his mother and sister at lunch; but it was silly of them all to let politics interfere in this way with family business. *Talking of business,* the note continued, *I have to get to Birmingham for first thing tomorrow morning. I'll drive over tonight and look up an old chum. Be back some time on Sunday. Yr loving Roly.*

In her bedroom, Mrs Covington opened the drawer of the bureau where she kept letters and placed his on top of the pile that represented a sort of layered fossil record of her life. At the very bottom were small, almost square yellowed envelopes with the purple and indigo official rubber stamps of the Army post office and censors. These were Alfred's letters home from the ordnance supply base in France. Awkward, tender, they asked for news of 'little Roly' and 'baby Evelyn'. The letters began in 1915 and continued until he came back to England at the Armistice. There were only a few later letters from him; brief notes scribbled on hotel letterheads when he had been out of town on business. But for most of the post-war years they had been together all the time. Long ago, sentimentally, she used to think how nice it would be if he would write her a letter, even a short note, expressing his love for her. But, then again, why should he, when she never wrote him one? But every year or so, she reread those wartime letters. They seemed from a totally different man than the one who rapidly put on weight in the twenties, who grew a firm bristled moustache, who found India too hot, too Indian, who did the *Times* crossword every evening after the Second War, and who died, leaving her, two children, and no other evidence or consequence of his existence.

The next layer was formed from the dutiful letters that Roland had written from school. Here, in the boy's slightly cruel, sarcastic way, were the first mentions of Mr Henry. Then came home-made Christmas and birthday cards made by the infant Evelyn. A few more, increasingly perfunctory letters from Roland short of money before the war, in the Army, and short of money again after the war. A selection of whining letters from Evelyn about the horrors of bringing up a child in rationed, Socialist England and the idleness

— even if enforced — of her crippled husband.

She closed the drawer on their voices.

This bureau was huge, pot-bellied, and full of secrets. It had been one of the few pieces of furniture that Alfred loved. Someone must have had it shipped out to India in the early part of the century; Alfred had shipped it back to England, at huge cost. It was the repository of his life's work for the bank, then the reliquary of all the useless occupations of his retirement: the angry correspondence regarding the fouling by dogs of the streets of Shrewsbury, published in the *Shropshire Bugle*; the small collection of valueless Roman coins; the pamphlets and newsletters of the Friends of St George, a rival organisation to the League of Empire Loyalists. She had kept up his subscription; the literature still arrived bearing his name. It was a sort of memorial, she supposed. And somebody had to help support their work or the whole Imperial idea would dissolve away, and the Socialists and their mean, envious little world would have triumphed for ever. Three guineas a year was a small price to pay for that. Which reminded her — their quarterly journal, *The Patriot*, was late in arriving. As with everything else, even the supporters of the good were becoming terribly lax.

It was a pity that Roland had never known India. That was the tragedy of his life, though he didn't seem to recognise the fact. When they had gone out in '35, he was already a grown man of twenty-three. As far as he was ever a grown man. He could have come over, but he was always full of excuses. The richest had been that he was getting married. Better to say that he was going to have to get married. Roland would have cut quite a dash in India, certainly more so than Evelyn ever did, with her regrettable sergeant. Her injured sergeant. Evelyn was not the sort to be able to deal with things like that. Why should she be expected to? Duty, of course. Mrs Covington herself had nursed Alfred through those last gruesome weeks. It had been a merciful release when he had gone. For all of them.

★ ★ ★

The letter addressed to James came at noon the next day, Saturday. His Aunt Evelyn told him of its arrival. An unwarm smile flickered over her thin lips. 'I don't know what it is,' she sniffed, 'but it may be what you are waiting for.' She seemed irritated that the world outside the garden had somehow infiltrated into the house.

199

A large brown envelope lay on the rent table. The writing of the name and address was his grandmother's; the postmark of the village in Devon. He opened it. Inside was a small piece of blue notepaper and another envelope, this one long, buff, stamped OHMS.

The note first: *Dear James, Here is the notice, I think, though of course I haven't opened it, of your National Service call-up. We do wish you well. You must write as soon as allowed. With all love from Nanna and Granddad.*

The contents of the buff envelope were more formal. He was to report to RAF Padgate. A rail travel warrant to Warrington — but from, irritatingly and uselessly, Exeter — was enclosed. There were instructions as to what articles he should bring with him. He was to arrive on Thursday the 9th of August, 1956. Today was Saturday — he had less than a week. Where was Padgate? Warrington?

Julia was sitting in the garden.

'It's come,' he said.

'What? Your letter. Oh, no. You've only been here a few days.'

'It's taken a week to get here from Devon.'

'When do you have to go?'

So, it was agreed between them that this was a small tragedy. James sat down, across the iron garden table. They faced the sky over Wales; the clouds high and moving fast. The sun fleeted across the lawn, the table and their faces. His wore a slightly comic, rueful smile as he reread his official letter.

'As they say,' said James, 'it's an ill wind. At least I shall be away and doing something. Not stuck here or at some dreary university.'

'I thought you liked it here.'

'Please don't get me wrong. I didn't mean anything. I do really like it here. When you're here.'

'I'm always here.' She laughed.

'Yes. That's half the trouble.'

'Trouble?'

'No — not trouble.' His face went red. 'It's just that it will be hard to leave you. We've only known each other such a short time. You are my cousin, after all.'

'I'll be sorry when you have to go.'

The clouds opened and closed again and the sunlight swept across the table followed by shadow, like curtains dividing the acts of a play, while they remained as silent as two actors: *They are seated, facing west. The same scene, moments later.*

★ ★ ★

Mrs Covington had had a small glass of wine at lunch and it was enough to send her sidling towards sleep. She tried to resist for a while. She lay back in the armchair and the contents of the room presented themselves in an odd, half-hallucinatory way as her eyelids shut and then opened again.

The Indian silver sweet dish on the broad upholstered arm of the chair held four of the five Craven A cigarettes she allowed herself per day. The Mughal painting, on linen, was faintly creased under the glass. It showed a prince and his consort, their heads haloed in gold, being borne in a palanquin by six bearers, through a stylised landscape of triangular shaped green trees and shrubs. She had never decided if she liked it or not. Her books. Alfred's books — Galsworthy, Anthony Hope, *The Business Encyclopaedia* in nine volumes, Cumber-Murray's *Tales from the Sanskrit*, Marshall's *The Island Race*, and all of Alfred's other impenetrable, never to be opened books on banking and law. She often thought they could be thrown out. But they were a world. The world that kept them all safe.

On that thought, she fell asleep, and slept through the showery afternoon.

★ ★ ★

Evelyn considered the arrival of her brother. She came to the conclusion that it was a bad thing. Already Roland's influence had begun to bend the manners of the household, and to corrupt its will. And James? The boy had clearly had an impact of some emotional sort on Julia. She was different, even day to day she changed. *O, brave new world, that has such people in it,* indeed! But it was a problem that Evelyn had to acknowledge at last, the problem of what was to be done with Julia now, and in the future. She was too pretty to remain ignorant for much longer of the effects of her looks on others. And she was too clever in a high-strung imaginative way to be very useful in a mundane job. So what was to be done with her? University was out of the question. Some role must be found for her; her duty lay in the family and in the house. Julia's grandmother would not live for ever, despite the signs of her clear intention to do so. Evelyn looked every day for signs of decay in the old lady, of slippage. There would be money when she had gone. They could shut up the house and she could take Julia out of the country and set up in some place where life was still decent and orderly. A place that knew its proper stations and orders and classes — and that knew how to keep them in place.

South Africa would be worth considering. She had heard good things of Cape Town. The climate was equable. There were servants to be had cheaply. White tablecloths that were replaced each day, silver regularly and properly polished and glinting in the perpetual, but benign sun. What was it called — Tablecloth Mountain? Because of the snow on its flat top. Something like that. The Boers, or whatever they were known as now, were pretty frightful, admittedly, but they had kept a grip. The rest of Africa, my God, the horror, the horror — all the utterly frightful things that were bound to happen when they got their blessed independence.

But perhaps this Suez business might prove to be the last straw even for this supine Conservative government. This might just be the turning point, when the people — the good people of England — would find their voice and the British lion would roar out a great, resounding 'NO' to these upstarts, babus, and savages . . .

The thought thrilled her. They had the might still. Two world wars had been fought and won, surely the defence of the Gate to the East would be simple in comparison to that? It was a pity that young James had to go into the Forces now. But it would get him away from the house. And he would acquit himself well. He had been to a good school. Rex would . . . Rex would have done well too. Given the chance. The coward . . .

* * *

Mr Henry looked down at the young people as they walked in the garden. They were talking earnestly. Julia halted and faced James, her mouth working. James nodded once, then shook his head vigorously from side to side. A disagreement, but not an argument. The girl was in a fawn raincoat; her dark hair tumbled over her shoulders, her eyes were bright. They reached the end of the lawn, turned and began their way back. The boy was handsome, in that rather unfocused, frowning, puzzle-faced way that boys of his age could be.

Mr Henry came away from the window and sat down in the Victorian rocking chair. As he did every day, increasingly and obsessively, he began to run through the possible versions of his future. There must be something he had missed, some clue as to how he could save himself, some miraculous lifeline that might be thrown to him.

There was nothing.

He had his old age pension. He pursed his lips in irritation. What a bitter term to use

— 'old age'. He who had been perennially youthful; who had been in love with youth. He looked nothing like his age, he was sure. He had the school pension too, for what that was worth. *In the circumstances, we do not feel that the payment of a full-term pension would be appropriate* . . . How much time did he have?

How much time? What time? Lately, he thought much about time and how inequitable and rather nonsensical the whole idea was. This freight of memories in his head; this load that he carried from one day to the next — what was that? The past grew more vivid and detailed, but every single day of his present existence seemed to grow more tedious and muddled. Yet the weeks and months and years went scurrying away; like that cliché of the cinema where the leaves of a calendar peel away in the wind. But the days of memory, the days of childhood and youth, they stood clear and shining, one by one. It was as if the past were becoming more real than the present, that it stood for ever, fixed, not part of the perpetual flux of life, that strange ribbon, whose unspooling could never be halted or apprehended. *Apprehended* in both meanings: to seize; or to hold in the mind, to understand. Did the past not die, then? Did it truly exist somewhere; unreachable of course, but real and solid and *going on*? And were not the past and the future implicit in the present? In the matter of this chair, in the fact that it existed, had existed, had continued to exist while he sat in it? Five minutes ago he had sat down, and the future was implicit in him and in the chair, in the fact that they were still here, five minutes later. This was the future that the chair had promised five minutes ago, or a year or twenty years ago. So, did that not mean that the future too must already exist, that past and future are one continuum, with the past manufacturing the future? The one time which did not exist, the one which was purely illusory, was the one that was supposed to be the most obviously provable — the Present. It could be argued, some of the Greeks had argued it, that there was no such thing as 'time'. The perceived flowing of a river of time was illusory; the measurement of it by clocks and calendars was arbitrary. The original Old English word *tima*, came from the same root as 'tide' — the ebb and flow of the sea. Just a pulse of the earth and sea, then. Time does not exist. There is no flow of time; it is just a kind of constant re-placement of the world. Then why, he thought bitterly, looking at the mottled, liver-spotted backs of his hands, why am I so bloody old?

He sat on, bewildering himself.

Time passed.

Or, rather, the past accumulated behind him, and the future quietly devoured the afternoon.

PART THREE

1

For the rest of the weekend, Evelyn observed the two. James and Julia sat at the iron garden table, talking, talking for hours, earnestly, each with one hand on the table. At times they came close to touching, then the hands would be withdrawn suddenly, as if frightened by the nearness of intimacy.

Roland came back on Monday. His clothes were crumpled, his face puffy. 'Bloody good weekend,' he said leeringly when Evelyn asked him sarcastically if he had had a good time.

He joined the children in the garden. From behind the lace curtains of her room, Evelyn watched them. When Roland sat down at the table everything changed; it was like a stone being thrown into a pool. James sat back, listening to his father, but glancing every now and then at Julia. And Julia would somehow gather into herself, wrapping her arms around her, shifting away from Roland. For Julia did not like Roland, Evelyn could see that, and it gave her some satisfaction. His charm obviously hadn't worked on this occasion. And Margaret had left him too. It

211

had taken her long enough. Evelyn looked forward to her brother leaving the house for good. Surely he did not intend to spend the rest of the summer here? By Wednesday she was tired of watching them all.

★ ★ ★

On Wednesday, after lunch, James was disappointed to see his father again come through the windows and head over to their table. He was carrying a glass of wine. But the first thing he said was encouraging.

'Haven't got long, I'm afraid. Got to see a man at the Dog,' he said. 'Hope to see you tonight, old chap. But if you're packing for tomorrow, let me give you a word of advice . . . '

His father warned James not to take too much. He would soon be in uniform anyway, and from that point on he could consider himself dead — or, at least non-existent — as a civilian, or as a sentient, discrete — Roland rolled the 'r' in a thin dismissive rasp — human being. For six weeks or so he would disappear into the maw of basic training, to be spewed forth as a private soldier — or whatever they called them in the Air Force. Didn't pay to look too soft or prosperous anyway. Marked man. So, bare essentials only, okay? He drained his wine glass. Sorry he had to barge off. James didn't fancy one himself, did he?

'I have to be up very early tomorrow, Dad,' James said pointedly.

'Absolutely. Don't tell your dear aunt where I've gone. Mum's the word. What's Dad, after all? The one who keeps mum. See you later, kiddies.'

When he had gone back into the house, James wanted to take Julia's hand and say he was sorry, that his father wasn't always like this, wasn't always as awful as this. She seemed to be deliberately looking away from him, at nothing in particular, just away from him. Surely she must know that there was nothing in common between him and his awful father?

'Why didn't you go down with him for a drink?'

'This is my last day. I don't want to spend it in a pub with Dad.'

'No.' She paused. 'How do you want to spend it then? It seems such a waste not to do something.'

'I suppose so.'

'Mother won't do anything to mark your day, nor Grandmother.'

'We — ' He felt as if he were trying to swallow a hard ball of something. ' — We

213

could do something. Together. In the village . . . '

'I told you, I never go to the village.'

'I don't mean to the pub. There's the cinema.'

'There isn't one.'

'Yes, there is. Beside the garage. It's only a little flea-pit, but it looks fine.'

'I didn't know. But Mother wouldn't have let me go even if I had known.'

'How old are you?'

'You know how old I am.'

'You're almost eighteen. I asked my father.'

'How did he know?'

'He is your uncle. Uncles know about birthdays, don't they?'

'He's never sent me a birthday card or anything,' she said.

'I think we should go down to the village. I think we should go to the cinema. I think you should go out.'

'I'll have to ask my mother.'

'No.' The word came out almost as a wail. 'No,' he said, quietly this time. 'We'll just go. There's no harm in it. I don't understand your mother. This house. I don't understand any of it. There's nothing here, is there, if you're young?'

'Don't criticise my mother, I've been very happy here.'

'All I'm saying is this — this is my last night here for some time. I wanted to spend the evening with you.' For the first time his hand reached all the way across the table and was laid gently on hers. Her hand did not move.

'All right, I'll ask her.'

He pressed her hand. 'No,' he said gently. 'If you ask her, she'll say no.'

'Why?'

'Don't you think she will?'

'Probably.' She gazed at their lightly linked hands as if not sure what they were. 'All right,' she said. 'What shall we do?'

The second house was at eight-thirty, he said. He had been down to the village earlier to check. They could slip away after dinner. They would use the gate at the end of the garden. No one would see them.

★ ★ ★

'This is the last night that we shall see James for a little while. He is away from us tomorrow, taking — if I may say so — the first step on the path to manhood.'

Mrs Covington raised her eyebrows.

Mr Henry, unnoticing, went on, 'I remember my own entry into the field in the First World War, and your father's,' he

215

nodded gravely to James, ' — your father's in the Second. God forfend that the present troubles presage a third such conflict. But,' his fingers grasped the stem of his wine glass, 'I hardly think that such grave thoughts should lie upon us on such an occasion. In short — '

'Thank God for that,' said Roland.

'In short,' said Mr Henry, now a little flustered, 'a toast. To Peace. To Youth. To James.'

Peace. Youth. Peace. James. Youth. The words collided with each other from their responses. Roland refilled his glass. The others sipped at their claret; Mr Henry merely wetted his lips, to impress with his self-control.

The toasts over, Julia asked if she might be excused. She had a slight headache. James said he had to go and pack for the morning. At just after eight o'clock, they met in the garden.

★ ★ ★

They walked through the village. The sun was descending behind the hills, but the cloud had cleared and the sky was blue above them. The roofs were still wet after a shower and the light had made them glisten, but evening

216

was beginning to rise in the alley beside the church. As they went through the churchyard, the gravestones were grey and grey-blue and shadows were gathering in the incised letters. They came out on the green. The windows of the Dog were bright, holding a sort of puppet show of heads and hands lifting cigarettes and glasses.

The path across the village green ran diagonally from corner to corner. In the middle, three boys leaned against the iron rail that ran round the pond. In front of them, two girls, perhaps fourteen years old, threw a ball intently and deliberately between them, one holding the ball to her chest and intoning some charm, before releasing it back to her friend, who would do the same, with some answering verse, and then send the ball back. The boys leaned in an exaggerated way on the rail, their legs stretching across the path. Julia said, 'Which way is it to the cinema?' hoping they could avoid the boys and girls. But James struck out towards them.

The ball went this way and that across the path. The soft chanting went into the evening air, then stopped. James strode a little way ahead, Julia hurried behind. He came level with the girls. Almost at the last moment the ball stuck in the hands of the fair-haired girl. She smiled faintly at James. The path was narrow, it would have been easy to step on to the grass, but James stopped in front of the boys.

'Excuse me, may we get by?' he said loudly.

Slowly the boys straightened, withdrawing the barrier of their legs slowly. Their eyes were fixed on the houses opposite. As they went a few steps past, one of the boys said, 'Tha's that mad girl.' James stopped and turned stiffly, bristling like a dog at a challenge. But the three boys had turned their backs and were studying the pond with great interest. The ball went pit-pat, back and forth; the soft chant began again.

Julia said lightly, 'Come on, James. We'll be late.' She took his hand and squeezed it. Did she imagine that, from one of the boys came a whispered parodic echo, *Oh, come on James. We shall be late*, in a high, mock-educated voice.

The tiny cinema, inaptly titled The Grand, was between the post office and Wilkinson's Garage.

'The last time I went to the pictures the place was absolutely enormous,' said Julia.

A small house rather, turned sideways on and with a whitewashed plaster portico of two fat Doric pillars on either side of open double doors.

A tiny woman sat in a tiny kiosk; only the

top of her head was visible above the counter. The tickets came off a cloakroom roll; the money went into an open drawer that contained only a handful of silver and copper coins.

Beyond the double doors were two heavy black curtains. They went through. A film was showing already on the square screen.

Laurel and Hardy were standing on a snowy street. Oliver was plucking at a double bass and singing in his rich, cordial tenor, while Stan chirped a bird-like counterpoint. A hat was on the pavement.

There could not have been more than twenty rows of bucket seats, eight on each side of the central aisle. They sat halfway down and the reflected light from the screen flickered over their faces. James snatched a glimpse of Julia, her lower lip caught in a moment of delight by her white teeth as she watched Stan trying to fry fish using the iron spring of a rooming-house bed as a grill.

When the short finished, they had the news. The clipped cut-glass voice of the commentator barked over images of grey warships, bucking up and down in a grey, rolling sea under a grey sky — 'Our boys at Sea — and on Land' — a view of boots, boots, boots clumping down, grinning faces with bad teeth under helmets and berets — 'and in the Air' — a flight of Meteor jets climbed swiftly and arced away from each other like a giant black and white firework going off — 'all ready in case the balloon goes up.'

'Mr Henry should be reading this,' James whispered.

She laughed.

'Shush,' said someone behind them. The reek of orange peel and the crackle of sweet papers came from the same direction.

The main feature film was *The Day the Earth Stood Still*. A film for children almost, Julia thought at first. The great silver spaceship, the giant protective robot, the ridiculous guns of the military powerless against the metal of the ship. But then she was so used to a static world that to be invited into the illusory black and silver depths of Washington streets, to witness the warmth of another household, all of this was enthralling.

It was over too soon. They stood up to leave, waiting through the playing of the National Anthem. The ceiling lights, like a few symmetrically laid out stars, warmed through dull orange to dim yellow. The anthem crashed tinnily to its end and they made their way up the aisle. The green lit clock showed ten forty-five.

Other patrons stood on the pavement outside. An old man said 'Goodnight,' to Julia, tipping his trilby hat. A middle-aged couple, clutching a large paper bag, presumably full of orange peel and sweet wrappers, hurried past, glancing at them with suspicion. A few more dissolved into the warm, damp summer night. Then no more.

Only one light was showing in the Dog, softly illuminating the bottles behind the bar. A woman lifted an empty pint glass quizzically in front of her face, then delicately applied a white cloth to its interior.

The centre of the green was in darkness that the street lamps did not reach. They recrossed the green. The boys and girls had disappeared. James and Julia came to the passage between the churchyard and the rectory walls. The house stood about a hundred yards from the other end. The night was very dark, the stars and any moon above were obscured by cloud.

When they came to the gates, the light from the hall shone brightly through the fanlight.

'Oh God, they're still up,' said Julia.

'Don't worry. It's perfectly all right.' James took her right hand and squeezed it to encourage her. Her fingers first closed on his, then pulled gently free as they walked up to the house.

Julia had not thought that the front door would be locked. She tried the handle. 'We shall have to wake them up,' she said despairingly.

'No. Dad will only just have got back from the pub, I bet.' James lifted the brass lion's-head knocker and rapped twice, as quietly as he could, and then once more, as if giving a prearranged signal.

The door was opened very quickly — by Mr Henry, who must have been waiting like a porter on the other side.

'Miss Julia!' His face was a mask of concern behind the torch that he waggled absurdly in their faces. 'Where on earth have you been? Your mother — '

'Is that her? Is that her?' her mother's voice shrieked from the sitting room. It was, Julia thought many years later, rather like seeing Mrs Rochester appear in *Jane Eyre*. Her mother's face was pale and angry.

'Where on earth have you been?' She advanced as Mr Henry shut the front doors behind them.

Enhancing the illusion that they were all taking part in a play, or comic opera, Roland appeared behind her. The cigarette between his lips wagged up and down as he spoke.

'Your dear mother was on the brink of sending Mr Henry to the phone box on the green for the police.'

'What else was I supposed to do?' It was plain that an argument had been taking place between the two.

'I should think that they would simply have laughed at you.'

'Don't be absurd.'

'I really don't think you should address Mrs Walters in that way, Mr Roland.' Mr Henry was shaking — in rage or fear — when he burst out with this, astonishing them all.

'Oh, shut up, *Mister* Henry,' said Roland. 'For God's sake, a girl of eighteen is out at ten o'clock in the evening — great tragedy.'

'She is not a girl — not of that sort,' said Evelyn.

'Mother had the right idea,' he said. 'She simply went to bed and left you to it.'

'Where then have you been?' Evelyn at last managed to round on her daughter again.

'To the cinema.'

'The cinema? What cinema?'

'The cinema in the village,' said Roland. He had fetched his drink and leaned against the door frame of the sitting room. 'You know perfectly well that there is a cinema in the village.'

She wheeled round to face him. 'I know

nothing of the sort. What interest to me is it if there is such a place?'

'Oh — you're priceless. If I were you, Julia, I'd just hop off to bed. And you James. Bad lad, indeed.'

'I am absolutely furious, Roland, that your son should take it into his head to persuade Julia to leave the house, secretly, furtively, without asking my permission or saying where they were intending to go.'

'I'm terribly sorry, Aunt — ' James began.

Roland cut him short. 'Don't apologise. Julia is eighteen.'

'She is seventeen,' said Evelyn.

'Seventeen, eighteen — she's of age.'

'What for?'

'Legally she's of age. Age of consent.'

'Don't be filthy.'

Roland laughed and shook his head in mock disbelief.

'Priceless. Priceless,' he gasped.

'I am going to bed,' Evelyn announced icily. 'We shall get no further with you clowning about. I will speak to you in the morning, Julia. You will be leaving tomorrow, James, I know that. I wish you well if I do not see you then. But I must say that I regard your conduct concerning Julia to be quite outrageous.'

'They are cousins,' said Roland.

'Consanguinity — '

'Shut up, Mr Henry.'

Mr Henry said only, 'If I may . . . ' He walked to the library door and went in, closing it softly behind him.

'I suggest you go to your room, Julia,' said her mother. 'As I say, I shall be interested to hear your explanation in the morning.'

'I'd swear that my dear sister is secretly enjoying herself immensely.'

'Goodnight,' said Evelyn with great dignity.

'Goodnight, kids,' said Roland, following uncertainly in his sister's wake.

Julia and James heard some muffled words exchanged on the gallery above, then the slam of a door. Roland appeared, leaning over the balustrade.

'Goodnight, kiddies,' he said, and saluted them grandiosely with his glass.

2

RAF Padgate
Sunday, 12th August 1956

Dear Julia,

I'm sorry I haven't written before. I simply
haven't had a chance to sit down, let alone
write a letter. Everyone is absolutely
exhausted with all the work and the
upheaval of life. I am in a hut with about
thirty other men. I feel a bit sorry for some
of the younger chaps — well, we're all
about the same age, but you know what I
mean, I think — some are very boyish and
have never been away from home or
roughed it before. There was one crying on
the first night a couple of beds away from
me.

You know that Dad ran me up from the
house to the station at Shrewsbury. That
was pretty early and I had to change at
Manchester. You could spot us all up and
down the train by a sort of frightened look.
We steamed into Warrington about 7 a.m.
in the end. There were lorries waiting and
by the time we got to the camp there were

quite a few people there still in civvies and they said they'd had breakfast already and that it had been awful. Well it was — but only as bad as school, which was pretty bad.

This is only a kitting-out camp and that's what they did with us. A ghastly medical I won't go into. Sorry — we swore an oath to the Queen first, I didn't mention that. Then the haircut — you won't recognise me now. Shorn lambs. We had to go along a very long counter for kit. As you go you have to shout out your size for shirts and hat and whatever and they slap it down on the counter. It sort of fits. Then tests and jabs and they ask you if you want to do an extra year, if you would like to sign up for another year. Well, no, frankly. And they know the school you're from and ask if you are interested in trying for a commission. Again, I said no. Do you think I'm being very silly and awkward? I don't think so. I never asked to be here and I'm prepared to do my duty, but I can't say I particularly care for the thought of ordering people to kill other people. Things aren't as clear as people try to make out. Forgive me — but your mother and grandmother are so wrong about all this Suez business. Of course a lot of people here are gung-ho about it, but quite a few of the chaps have their doubts. I can't help but feel that your folks tend to live in the past. Don't let them drag you there or keep you there. Am I being awful?

I hope you didn't get into too much hot water after the other night. It was all quite innocent. Your people really are quite extraordinary.

I'll write again. We're being shipped out of here on Tuesday — to Credenhall. That's not too bad at all. It's near Hereford and you are not so far away. I shall have a leave straight after basic training, which should fall around the 28th or 29th of next month. But, as I say, I'll write again. I hope we're friends. The thought of you keeps me sort of happy and sane and ready to go on. Do you understand? Don't please write back just yet. As I say, we're on the move soon. I'll write and give you the address to write to. If you want to, of course.

Yours,
James

Evelyn knocked, waited for her mother's answer, and went in.

Mrs Covington stood by her bureau, pulling on a pair of black gloves. 'Am I late?' she asked cheerfully.

'Not quite yet.'

'You're always ready far ahead of time, Evelyn. I really don't see the necessity. Besides, I felt a little unwell. I'm slowing down terribly this past year.'

Evelyn searched her mother's face for signs of quickening mortality. Was she paler, her skin drawn tighter?

'Oh dear,' she said. 'Would you rather not come today?'

'No, no. Especially today. Do you realise, Evelyn, that it was almost fifty years ago on this date, a Saturday then, that I was married? And I should have sent the Reverend Purvis a note to ask him to mention James in prayers, now that the boy is off to fight for Queen and Country.'

'I don't think that would be altogether ... I don't know. I told you about his conduct on Wednesday night.'

'That was a relatively minor matter, if you don't mind me saying so, Evelyn. The girl has got to start going out sometime. You can't keep her locked away for ever.'

'It's not a matter of locking her away.'

'And what about you? You never go anywhere or do anything — apart from that wretched holiday every year that you never enjoy. You should get married again.'

'What about you? Who's to look after you

— and the house?'

'I had rather thought it was the other way round,' Mrs Covington said sharply. 'Anyway, this house is far too big for just the two of us. I've been thinking about it.'

'There's Julia as well. And Mr Henry.'

'Julia won't stay. Not when she tastes the world. And Mr Henry can't stay.'

'Where is he to go?' Evelyn sounded puzzled.

'He can't stay for ever, Evelyn. His job's done . . .'

Evelyn opened the bedroom door. 'We'd better hurry,' she said.

'We can't keep him on purely out of sentiment, like a pet dog . . .'

* * *

Mr Henry was halfway out of his door when he heard some of this. He retreated back inside, his heart pounding. The time had come. His time had come. He trembled like a terrified hare.

* * *

So they set out, in procession, to the church built in the Conqueror's reign. Evelyn went in front. Behind her came Julia. And then Mr

Henry and Mrs Covington: Mr Henry gazing down anxiously at the pavement, to step the path out for Mrs Covington, whose hand rested on his arm and whose nose was lifted imperiously above all time and flux and the patch of chalky dog turds that Mr Henry guided her past with a gentle tug of the elbow.

The Conqueror's church? Yes, built then, and now half-filled with the descendants of the conquered — the farmers and labourers and postman and schoolteacher — whose local tongue almost overwhelmed the carefully tuned enunciation of the descendants of the conquerors — the families of Doctor, and Major-General, and the Covington brood — as they mingled lustily together in the first hymn, *New every morning is the love . . .*

* * *

One — almost — of the gentry, but agnostic and choosing to breakfast late, Roland sat in the kitchen, busying his face with ministrations of cigarette and coffee, and considering his lot, his fate, and his future. Certainly, if one chose to, one could live on very little, but one must live on something. At the moment the choice lay between working and the prospect of having nothing. Neither was exactly inviting. Better be dead than end up as some glorified bloody clerk. He'd seen it happen to too many good chaps after the war. What was it — 'sit on your arse for forty years and hang your hat on a pension'? No thank you. If there were still to be women and a drink or two and a few good suits, arrangements had to be made and made quickly.

Now — while they were all out of the house.

He knew where his future lay — in that bureau in his mother's bedroom. The question was, how long did he have to wait? How many years? Decades?

Time to get to it. Find out the state of play. He stubbed out his cigarette in the saucer and put his breakfast things in the sink. As he went across the hall he let his fingers trail lovingly over the beeswaxed top of the rent table. To guard against any unexpected early return from church, he bolted the front door.

He looked through the side window. Outside, a filmy drizzle was being blown about the garden. He mounted the stairs.

And stood in front of the bureau.

Ah, what a marvellously tempting array of drawers. He also knew — after years of prying when he was a boy — where the secret compartment was and what papers and documents it held.

He opened one drawer as an experiment. Ah yes, his memory held up — this one was just the same as ever; the personal letters of many years. He knew their contents off by heart. He amused himself for a moment or two by reading one of his own letters from school, then one of Evelyn's, whining about India and her marriage. No change there, then.

The configuration of the drawers devoted to business was not much altered. He opened and shut the one filled with old bills and receipts. Now, if nothing had changed, he should be able to pull out this central drawer, the one with, yes, cheque and deposit books and bank statements going back to the Ark, and pass his hand in and over the roof of wood at the back and there should be treasure. Ah, here it was — his fingers felt bundles of papers on the hidden shelf. He pulled them out; three bundles, tied with blue and red silk ribbons.

He arranged them on the blotter. The bundles did not seem as thick as he remembered them. Here were the papers concerning his father's estate, the paid out insurance policies, the will, the letters of attorney . . . all that was history. His mother's will, her insurance policies — none of these was changed. But here was a new packet of correspondence relating to mortgages on the estate farms. Some of these were only a few years old. With the first faintly sick feeling of unease he laid those to one side for further investigation. Where were all the share certificates? Where was that particularly plump and aesthetically satisfying bundle of engraved certificates from the blue chip companies in which his father had so cannily invested over the years? Roland had long looked forward to the day when regular plump dividends would fall through the letter box on to the hall floor of his house, and he could always be sure he could splash out every now and then by converting some to capital. He must have missed them. His fingers searched at the back of the drawer again, but encountered only rough, unplaned wood. He opened all the other drawers, his hands moving rapidly, lifting papers, glancing at them, then replacing them so expertly that no one could tell that they had been disturbed. Here were the accounts for the farms. The rents seemed to have been paid regularly, though this old custom of collecting them only once a year would have to change. Only one — Perkins — was in arrears. Perhaps he should call on old Perkins himself. But it was Michaelmas in six weeks' time. The rents would fall due for another year then. But the rents still seemed abnormally low, most of them at their pre-war rate. That too would have to change. The bills certainly hadn't remained the same. He hadn't got time to go through all those. He would have to risk it and take away all the documents from the hidden compartment so that he could read through them properly.

He took out the leather pouch of bank statements and extracted the two most recent. There didn't seem a lot in the current account. He carefully detached two cheques and their stubs from the book on the front of which his mother had written *Farm Accounts*. There was some money in that one and the last cheque had been written many weeks ago. It looked as if she used it only rarely. He smoothed everything back into its proper, remembered place and shut the drawer.

He sat down and gathered the slim bundles of papers from the blotter. For a while he sat with them in his lap, staring thoughtfully at the bureau. The sun came out and shone in between the curtains. His face was lit in the dressing-table mirror. Needed a shave — but business first.

Julia walked back from church, in company, but alone in her mind. She thought about James. She hoped he was all right, that nothing horrible was happening to him. Men lived in such a strange world, and one that was almost entirely separate from her own. But surely all women didn't live like her mother and her grandmother? Those girls who had been playing with a ball on the green — they were much younger than she was, but they had freedom. And the young women who went to church. You could hear some of them at the back giggle as the Covington party came in. Giggling at these old-fashioned clothes. Julia looked down with disgust at her long black coat, and her square-toed black shoes. And, there, just in front of her was her tutor, the suddenly absurd-seeming Mr Henry in his black Sunday suit, wing collar and watch-chained waistcoat. Well, some of the older farmers dressed like that, but they and their families, their wives and children and grandchildren, they all looked robustly of this world — not like characters escaped from a novel for the afternoon.

★ ★ ★

Another of the characters much preoccupied with himself was Mr Henry. He could not get those overheard words out of his head: ' . . . can't keep him . . . out of sentiment . . . like a dog . . . ' The future was bearing down on him like an express train. What was he to do? Perhaps Mrs Covington had not been referring to him at all, but to Roland. No, that was a straw not worth clutching on to. What was he to do? If it was a question of the expense? He was paid a mere pittance anyway. But at least he had a roof over his head and free food. Could he afford such things on his miserable pension? Yes, of a sort. But his comfort would be gone. His library. His garden. Wine. Perhaps, with Julia's education at an end, he could help in some other way. However menial, he would be willing to consider it. Yes, yes — he grew excited. He glanced down at Mrs Covington's claw-like hand clutching his arm. He supported her in one way, at least. And by offering his services about the house they could also dispense with the services of Mrs Fellowes. It would be a comedown, but when the devil drives . . . To offer to be a servant rather than a scholar — perhaps it would excite her pity. Her hand rested complacent and sexless, its blue veins like those in some strange ancient

237

mineral, rather than human skin.

He would compose a speech tonight and seek an audience with Mrs Covington tomorrow.

★ ★ ★

Mrs Covington did not think at all about Mr Henry. As they came near to the house the vision of four remaining cigarettes in the box on her dressing table was held comfortingly in her mind.

★ ★ ★

It was late that night before Roland trusted the house was sufficiently at rest so that he could begin work. Dinner had passed with much less drunk than normal. Julia had — quite bizarrely, to him — asked his permission to write to James. He had smiled and found himself watching her as she walked away. He shouldn't think of her in that way. She was his niece, after all. But really, God knows, you couldn't help but notice how beautiful the girl was. How you got from Evelyn to her daughter was another of life's mysteries. Evelyn was one of nature's reconstituted virgins. Perhaps the daughter's looks came from the father's side. Old Rex had been all right. But Julia *was* odd; graceful and sweet-tempered, but so quiet. And she and James — it was quite laughable to contemplate. The sweet virgins. Well, life would solve those problems for them — the sweetness and the innocence.

Now, he hoped, they were all asleep. Poor bloody James in some godforsaken barracks. He felt for him. Roland had bought a bottle of whisky in the village yesterday and he poured himself a decent-sized slug. A chair placed under the doorknob secured it against surprise invasion. The war died hard, eh? A calming cigarette; he sat on the edge of the bed and began to lay out the papers taken from his mother's bureau.

It took him a good three hours to get a reasonably complete picture of her affairs. It was after one. He had broken out into a cold sweat when the truth began to dawn on him. But a couple of drinks straightened him out, that and a few more cigarettes. There was no doubt about it though, life was going to be a damned sight harder than he had dared to think.

Roland had always enjoyed himself safe in the knowledge that there was Mother, and when there wasn't Mother any longer, there would be the house and the estate and the money. There had been no need of a career or anything tedious like that. He had reached the age of forty-four waiting for life to begin.

All at once, the promise of that life seemed to have been withdrawn.

The farm bank account was down to a couple of thousand. The statements showed that large repayments had to be made every month on mortgages taken out on the estate farms over the past ten or so years. The only money coming in regularly was Mother's pension from the bank. There was no sign of any recent share dividends of any size. The only share certificates left were piddling, worthless ancient issues. Most of the insurance policies had been cashed in, or the premiums had not been kept up and the policies had lapsed. Any still in place were only payable on his mother's death, and the debts of the estate would swallow up their profits. In all, in fact, when his mother died the debts would outweigh any assets. And God alone knew what death duties would be levied on the notional value of the estate. The house would have to be sold. And the farms. But they were not even owned, were they? Whatever little was left would have to be divided between himself and Evelyn. Julia? He hunted for the will among the spread papers. Julia was to receive two thousand. As was James. They'd be lucky. He felt bitter towards his mother. She'd been selling off his birthright bit by bit, to keep her own mouldering life, or illusion of life, in place. His hands were shaking. For the first time in his life he felt afraid. It was as if a great, profoundly dark abyss had opened at his feet and he was forced to stare down into it and to see that this was his life from now on. He had achieved nothing. Nothing could now be done. *Steady on, old chap,* he whispered. Can't give up now. Didn't in the war, and what was this compared to that? He searched his mind for evidence of his previous bravery. Half-satisfying examples floated out of the past. That time in France, for instance, when they'd come under fire from some German 88s. He had flinched — first time in action and all that — but he'd done his bit, rallied the boys. Well, had the sergeant rally the boys. Then that bloody troopship in the Channel; he was one of the few who hadn't been sick. And he had helped Flatteau out just after the war when things could have got very nasty for him with those tough boys from Camberwell. You needed courage too to run an illegal betting book, and he'd done that for nearly a year at the Anchor. He had been resourceful. Made money here and there. Bit of a wastrel, bit of a charmer — he'd just have to try and cut back now. But he had — he knew he

241

had — bags of the old charm. That must be made to count for something. All he needed was enough capital to set him up in some small venture or other.

Decision time.

There was a heavy Victorian washstand in the corner of the room. He went over and removed the jug and placed it on the floor. Then he carried the heavy stand over to the bed. He would need a steady surface. He looked for something flat to put over the basin. In the bookcase by the door were some large old green volumes, *The Library Shakespeare*. He used one as his desk.

His mother's signature was easy enough, regularly displayed over various documents, a copperplate *E.B. Covington*. He practised it on the back of an old letter that was of no consequence and could be destroyed. He started with the handwriting he would need to match the signature. *One hundred pounds. Two hundred and eighty-three pounds only. Pay cash. Pay cash. Pay cash.* He did these over and over until he was sure his hand would work in the proper rhythm. Then he made out a cheque for three hundred and fifty pounds. That was the amount drawn on the last cheque. It was better that it looked like a regular withdrawal. He signed it with probably the worst of all his efforts. But it would pass. The writing calmed him down. He would keep the other cheque in reserve. He drew on his cigarette and held the smoke in for longer than usual, then blew out slowly. The whisky was taking hold of him. He would have one more for bed and keep enough for a livener in the morning. He must put the papers back in the old girl's bureau tomorrow. All this time, he was thinking something else out too. The only other money available was the rent due from the farms at Michaelmas. September the twenty-ninth. His pocket diary told him that this was on a Saturday this year. Perfect. Just have to get through until then.

3

The Round House
15th August 1956

Dear James,
It was wonderful to receive your letter. You haven't yet given me the address of the new camp but I've addressed this to you at RAF Credenhall and I hope it will reach you. (That's a silly sentence to write actually, isn't it? If you don't receive this letter, you will hardly be in a position to read it, will you?)

Everything is much the same here. Though something seems to have happened to Mr Henry. It is very strange. A week or so ago he suddenly started really sucking up to Mother and Grandmother, constantly asking if he could do this or that in the house. Quite menial things, like washing up or sweeping or dusting. And they are letting him do them! Grandmother has let Mrs Fellowes go and says that we can't afford staff. But it hardly seems fair on poor Mr Henry. He is my tutor after all, and to put him in an apron and make him do the housework does seem ridiculous. It certainly is very odd and slightly comical to see him wielding a broom, or putting out laundry to dry.

Since her outburst about the cinema, Mother has hardly spoken to me. What am I to do? I'm told I'm not to take a job. That isn't *at all* what they had in mind for me. But when I try to find out what I am to do, she says simply that I am not old enough to do anything. But I'm eighteen years old in November — and there you are, the same age practically, and you are away in the Air Force and seeing something of life.

I hope you are well and safe. All of that trouble over Egypt seemed to have died down, but now has reared its head again. You won't have to get involved, will you? Mr Henry still reads us the news every day, and every day it seems that there are ships sailing, or aeroplanes flying to the Middle East. Mother says that we 'have to show the flag', but it's very unlikely she would ever have to wave it.

The weather is getting better and warmer. Well, you must know that. I keep forgetting that you are not so very far away. I have enclosed a book, a present from Mr Henry. It's *A Shropshire Lad* by A. E.

Housman. He says it will cheer you up. Mr Henry was telling me about his own days as a soldier. I can hardly picture him in uniform, can you? I imagine you look most dashing and handsome in yours. Is it blue? When you come home — I mean, when you come here — will you be able to wear it? Everyone is very proud of you.

I did like our night out.

Please do write back if you get the chance.

Yours,
Julia

29th August 1956
Dear Johnny,

Long time no speak, eh? Bet you thought the old bastard was dead! Well, not much to say. I'm still stuck up here in this godforsaken hole with sister and old Mum. As entertainment value goes it ain't the Windmill. But things will move — the ice will break, my caravan, having rested, will move on, as it were. That business we were discussing — that's still on, is it? Just that I might happen to have the wherewithal before long to keep my end up. Patience, O wise one. Seriously, things could be on the up soon and no more buggering about.

Hope you and the good lady are keeping well. I was going to say wish all the boys and girls in the Anchor well too. But, on second thoughts, no . . . There are one or two in there who would not make me welcome — until I came across with the necessary to clear my fair name.

I'll keep in touch. As I say, that business — I'm serious, you know.

Toodle pip
Roly

4th September 1956
My dear Bertram,

It may come as some surprise to you to receive a communication from such a neglectful correspondent as your remiss and remorseful cousin.

The last time that we met must be almost twenty years ago now. Do you remember my father's funeral? It was an exceptionally severe day for the time of year, April the 25th, if I remember correctly. There was snow on the very morning of the funeral and we had to have a cab for Mother and some other ladies, including your own dear mother, my Aunt Margaret.

I recall well you asking my advice about an idea that you had for setting up a school in Eastbourne to 'cram' boys for the Common Entrance. I was glad to give you my thoughts and can only hope they bore some fruit. For I do know that you did succeed in establishing such a school shortly afterwards. At the time that we discussed your ideas, you were kind enough to say that a person such as I might very well make an ideal member of staff. As you know, I was then a house master at Cheshurst and unable to take up your kind offer. However, I have now been away from Cheshurst for this six years or more. At present I am employed as personal tutor to a family in the West Country. However, it being in the nature of young people to grow, this position is, of necessity, of limited duration.

I shall soon be able to reconsider my position here and begin to make plans for my future. I am still, I feel, a most youthful and energetic person despite the number of years that I have steadily accumulated. For, over those years, I have also accumulated knowledge and, if I may say so without appearing immodest, a certain amount of wisdom. My subjects are primarily English and History, with

Classics a close third, but I can usefully turn my hand also to Mathematics, Geography and the Natural Sciences.

I do think, dear cousin, that we could very well work together. Perhaps I might visit you before the Christmas vacation to discuss this matter in greater detail?

I look forward to hearing from you.

Yours, most affectionately,

Douglas Henry (MA)

12th September 1956
Dear Mr Chapman,

I am writing to you and the other tenants to remind all on the estate that rents due for Michaelmas are to be paid, in cash, at the Round House, on Saturday, September 29th at any time between 10.00 a.m. and 3.00 p.m.

As usual at this time of year, I shall be most pleased to receive all tenants, their wives and children at a supper to be held in the garden of the Round House from 7.00 p.m. onwards.

I hope to see you all there.

Yours cordially

Beatrice Covington

16th September 1956
Dear Julia,

I'm sorry I haven't replied for so long. It is so strange that this camp is only twenty or thirty miles away from you — it is like being in another world.

We were treated quite well at Padgate when we were kitting-out. As I told you, I didn't put in for a commission, or for signing on for an extra year. You get the trade of your choice and more money, but I want to get out after two years.

Anyway, all that stuff was just a sort of preliminary softening up, because once we did sign up, everything changed. 'As you see,' said a chum I have made, George Tudor, 'the mask has slipped from our handlers.' He is a very decent type, a Welshman from the borders not far from you. But the mask did definitely slip. Where we had been asked politely to 'please fall in' by soft voiced SACs and Flight Sergeants, now the same men became like mad sheepdogs, snarling and snapping at our heels.

The whole thing continued when we got to Credenhall. From the moment when the board went down at the back of our truck we were screamed at and doubled here, there and everywhere. Drill, drill, march, march, polish, polish, clean, clean, loads of PE and walking along beams and struggling under obstructions. Some of the boys have found it much harder here.

The worst nightmare is to be selected for guard duty. Not so much for the duty itself — we have nothing in particular to guard — but for the preparations. You have to get into full uniform, which entails something really horrible called 'webbing'. Webbing is what you hang your water bottle and ammo and bayonet and full pack on. It's like a cross between a horse's harness and a nest of vipers and you need a couple of the other chaps to pull and push and pummel this mass of buckles and straps over and round you.

Guard duty itself is a farce. You are out in all weathers in the middle of the night and you simply march from this spot to that spot in the dark. The thing that you dread most is being challenged by the duty officer when he does his rounds. This involves a ritual exchange of challenges and responses not much less complicated, I should think, than High Mass. It takes some learning: 'advance and be recognised' sort of thing. I nearly wrote, 'you know the sort of thing,' but I'm glad you don't.

Anyway, this is all frightfully ludicrous because you have no sanction available to enforce your challenge. What I mean is, that if a real intruder broke into the camp and refused to obey you, you would have to get an officer's permission to take any action. As George Tudor said, it means that if Colonel Nasser is coming towards you, you have to ask him politely if he wouldn't mind standing there for a moment while you go off and get permission to come back and shoot him.

Apart from this it has been more drill — and ground combat training. This is walking over things and wading through water and crawling under things while thunder flashes go off by your ear. And lectures on hygiene and what our mothers never taught us — sorry — and religious education. But it'll soon be over.

In a week we complete basic training, then we have a drill competition to pick the best squad. Our sergeant, who is quite old and who is retiring this year, goes round saying he will hang himself if we don't win — but not before he has hanged the lot of us. Then we have the passing-out parade, then LEAVE!

I will have to go down and see my mother in London eventually, but I want to come to Driffold first and see you. Will they let me after all that fuss about the pictures?

Do write back and if the answer is yes to me coming, I shall see you as early as I can on Saturday the 29th.

All very best wishes

Yours

James

4

Michaelmas. Saturday the 29th of September, 1956.

Mr Henry had received an answer from his cousin. Unfortunately a trip to see the school would be futile; although no doubt desirable as a social call, there could be no question of a position of any sort being available.

We have room for ourselves — my wife and I — and the few boarders who come to us for special cramming. It is hardly a school as such . . .

The whole of the reply, which had been very short, read as if it was written to a stranger. So much for cousins. He looked down bitterly at the garden.

The green marquee stood on the back lawn. One of its opening flaps had been tied back and inside he could see the corner of one of the tables he had erected there yesterday. They were now all covered in white or yellow cloths and cutlery and small pots of flowers.

It was only nine in the morning and he was tired already.

Evelyn, crossing near the window in her bedroom to hang back a dress she had rejected for today, had a most odd turn. Out of the corner of her eye she saw the marquee, the lawn — and Rex. He stood between the guy-ropes, his red legs beneath khaki shorts, his sergeant's stripes on his shirt. He looked straight up at her and smiled.

She stood for a moment, then she squeezed her eyes shut and whispered, 'He is not a ghost.' She opened her eyes slowly, and he was gone.

★   ★   ★

Julia was unsettled. Over the past weeks she had found herself longing more and more to see James. At last he was coming back today. Things were intolerable. Her life was not her own. What could he do? Anything — anything to ease the situation.

What if he had to go away? If there was a war? According to Mr Henry, the Egyptians still posed the gravest danger. But it seemed to Julia that there was something ridiculous in his interpretation. How could the Egyptians have risen so suddenly and be so threatening, when only a few months ago they had been seen as among the most comical and helpless and hopeless of subjects, needing our help to do the slightest thing, unable to run the simplest undertaking in their own country, needing our firm hand to guide their affairs? How was it that they had now become such mighty and desperate foes — these wogs, as her mother witheringly called them? And poor James, now that he had finished his training, would be dragged into any war, wouldn't he? Uncle Roland had said that 'a company of Guards could sort that lot out quite comfortably', but that was by no means sure. And Uncle Roland also said the most impossible things simply, it seemed, to annoy Mother and Grandmother. Why were the women in this house so vengeful? There was almost a sense of savagery in their faces and voices when they talked of the 'wogs' and the Empire.

She stepped out of the kitchen door and into the garden. Uncle Roland was standing with his back to her. He was shouting to someone in the marquee that he didn't want the tables all bunched in the middle, but spread out.

He turned and saw her.

'Bloody yokels,' he said. 'I despair.' He tipped his head back and scanned the sky. 'Still, at least the weather may hold, eh? You ready? We'll make a move then.'

She followed him round the house to the car on the drive.

'I remember when you couldn't move in this garden for the Michaelmas party. Do get in. People knew who the Covingtons were then. Sad fall.' He accelerated out of the gates and on to the road. 'Not that we've fallen, eh, Julia. Just the family seems to be fading away. Got to expect it, I suppose. Things change. Times change. When I was in the Army in the war you could see that things had to alter. We were red-hot then for change. Hot Reds, almost. Voted Labour when I came back from Germany, I don't mind telling you. Confession's good for the soul. Don't tell your mother. Give her heart failure. I still haven't got back in their good books after that row about the Empire. Mustn't mind me, old girl.' He shot a quick glance sideways at her; she kept her eyes ahead. 'Just sometimes — ' He braked at a crossroads to let a horse-van go across. He accelerated away. 'Sometimes you have to — you get bored — don't know if you know what I mean — suppose you don't actually — but you have to change the old scenery around sometimes — as my old friend Morry Flatteau used to say. He was probably plastered at the time. But you know what I mean. Life has its ups and downs, but

257

it gets a bit tedious at times.'

'I know,' she said, but he didn't seem to notice.

'Take this Michaelmas do. I really hope it goes with a swing, what with young Jamie coming home and all.'

Julia didn't quite know what seemed wrong with James being called 'Jamie' by his own father, but she was surprised. There was more than a touch of sentimentality in the way that he said it; a whiff of that boozy camaraderie that hung around Uncle Roland like the smell of beer and stale cigarette smoke.

He drove silently then, as if digesting his own words. They were on the main road now, the Malverns over his right shoulder. Roland hummed to himself. Once or twice she felt him glance at her, but she pretended to study the view.

He spoke at last.

'I say, old girl, I get the impression you don't altogether approve of me. Your wicked uncle and all that? No? Not so bad as I'm painted.' He paused. 'By no means.' He hummed briefly again, then said, 'Be good to see old James again, though, won't it?'

'Yes, it will be,' she said carefully and regretted it at once, as sounding at the same time too prissy and too expectant. Why couldn't she ever get these things right?

'Station coming up. Yes. And there — unless I'm very much mistaken — is the son and heir himself.'

James looked taller and stronger. His bushy brown hair had been cut very short so that his ears looked disproportionately large. So did his hands, emerging from the blue cuffs of his uniform, and his feet, in comic black boots with highly polished toe-caps. A blue kitbag leaned against the wall behind him. He looked, thought Julia, very sweet.

★　★　★

Mrs Covington sat regally, or at least vice-regally, at the rent table, facing the open double front doors. She had ordered Mr Henry to open them at exactly ten o'clock to receive her tenants. She had composed herself; her half-moon reading glasses lay on the pages of the ledger before her. The doors were thrown wide. The drive was empty.

'Patience, Mr Henry,' she said. 'It is a fine day. Farmers are busy men. Please remain by the door to greet them.'

So, Mr Henry sat on a straight-backed chair by the side of the doors, feeling like a porter in a Russian novel, one of those servants who have nothing to do but sit by a door for fifty years and watch the entrances and deaths of the characters.

He examined the knees of his trousers. Was there a hint of the white of his leg through the cloth? Had the threads of his suit deteriorated to that extent? He had a faint buzzing noise in his ears and an ache in the lower forehead. These and other unpleasant feelings he experienced now most mornings, because for weeks Roland had regularly brought wine up from the cellar for dinner. His gaze wandered over the pictures on the walls. Landscape with haycart and small, rotund peasants. Blue-faced portrait of some non-relative of the Covingtons, left by the previous family. Cows, willows and stream. A reproduction of Chardin's *House of Cards*. A classical nude female, holding grapes aloft in one hand, clutching a marble pillar with the other. His eyes returned to Mrs Covington. She stared serenely down at the ledger.

★ ★ ★

'Mr Parchment.'

'Parchman.'

'I am so sorry. Parchman. I'm delighted to see you again.'

She extended a hand like a dead lily across the table and Mr Parchman shook it gently in his huge red fist.

'How is your family?'

'Well, thank you, Mrs Covington.'

'They will attend this evening?'

'As for the last fifty-two years,' he said.

'Good gracious.'

'Came here first as a boy with my father.' All the while he was talking, Mr Parchman had been producing, from a large canvas bag, many small brown paper bags full of coin and laying them carefully on the table.

'Values as marked,' he said. 'Tanners and shillings and florins and half-crowns. And the notes here.' From his inside pocket he brought out bundles of pound and ten-shilling notes, all more or less soiled. 'Two hundred and eighty pounds, seventeen and sixpence. I think you'll find that's correct, ma'am.'

'Of course. Never a penny out of place, Mr Parchman.' Mrs Covington smiled bleakly as she gathered the money to her with both hands. 'But I must admit you had me worried. I thought that you might be unwell.'

'I'm the last again then?' he said, and laughed in a not very convincing way.

'Yes, I'm afraid so.' Her blue veined hand placed the last bag in the copper drawer.

'Better late than never, though,' said Mr Parchman with the same strained joviality.

'I look forward to seeing you at our supper.'

'I wouldn't miss it for the world,' he said, recovering a little. 'And I hear your grandson is back. In the Queen's uniform.'

'Yes, James is back. And how are your children?' she asked, making a careful entry in the ledger.

'They're all grown.'

'Ah.' She looked at her watch. 'My goodness. It is past three. And you are the last, Mr Parchman. If you will excuse me.' She waved her left hand over the ledger as she shut it with the right, in a vague flourish, like a conjuror's.

Except that, Mr Henry thought, conjurors are always male, surely?

*　*　*

'I suppose I'll have to get changed.'

'Oh, surely not. I mean . . . '

'Well, washed.'

'You must wear your uniform. You've earned it.'

'I've never been to one of these parties. Dad was telling me about the old days. Huge parties.'

'Not really. They've always been the same.'

'I mean — when he was young.'

262

'Yes. Perhaps.'

'I saw the tent and tables and all. Looks quite a go anyway.'

How was it that his conversation excited her for a few moments, seemed to proceed in the way she was leading it, and then tailed off so feebly? He did look so nice in his uniform. She wished that he would kiss her. All he did was to reach in his pocket and bring out a packet of Players. He lit up and she was rather sad that he did it in such a matter-of-fact, knowing way, shaking the match out with his fingers extended, eyes screwed up — but then his face wore such a worried expression.

'I'm sorry — you don't mind, do you? All the blokes do. I got into the habit.'

'That's fine,' she said. 'Nothing ever really happens, you know, at this party. It's not terribly exciting.'

'What do they do?'

'There's never any music or anything. Grandmother lays it on every year and the tenants come because they have to, I suppose, but every year it seems to get that bit more dead.'

'Everything's dead here, Julia. I mean that. It's like an institution.'

'Don't be horrible,' she said. 'I know it's not what I like any more, but it's what I've got. You have to live with things.'

He said nothing. He should have said something.

* ★ ★

'What are you going to do with her then?' said Roland.

'Who?' said Evelyn.

'Julia. Your lovely daughter. What on earth do you have in mind for her?' From the dining room he could keep one eye on the hall. Mr Henry had just crossed over, his soft shoes flapping on the tiles, busy with preparations for the evening. The rent table was pregnant with the year's rents.

'And what about you?' he went on. 'You can't want to stick here for ever? You're too young to be on your own.'

'And you're too old to be on *your* own,' she said.

The words froze in the air between them. They both thought furiously that they meant well and both knew that they did not, in any way, mean well.

'I really cannot waste time talking to you,' said Evelyn. 'There is so much to be done.' Roland lit another cigarette. 'I suppose you'd better do it then, old dear,' he said.

'Why don't we carry it across to the tent?' James asked again. 'What else is there? It'll be utterly miserable without any music. What did you used to do?'

'It has fallen off over the last few years. I remember when I first came that we had a band from the village. It was the same people who did the marquee, but they don't come now.'

'Well, let's take the record player out.'

'I don't know. Grandmother's got older. There used to be a lot of beer, I think, and dancing. And Mother got not to like that. So, now it's really only the tenants and their families. A lot of the villagers have stopped coming.'

'That's what I mean — give them a surprise. Oh, come on, Julia. Nothing ever happens here.'

'But how do we get it out and over there? People will see us.'

'Not the people who care. We'll take it out by the windows.'

'What about the wires and plugs and things? They won't reach that far.'

'Leave that to me.'

When they carried out the gramophone, the whole house was quiet.

Roland had disappeared to the village, to catch the last half-hour in the pub after lunch. Evelyn was standing in the kitchen, watching Mrs Chapman, one of the tenants' wives, so that she didn't cut the cucumber too thick for the sandwiches. She had been told once, by an ex-Palace servant, the way that the Royal Family liked it to be done. The cucumber was first carefully peeled, then sliced in thin strips along the length of the cucumber, with the whole of the pulpy interior discarded. 'I should think,' the ex-servant had said proudly, 'that no member of the Royal Family has ever had to see a single cucumber seed.' But it was too late to stop Mrs Chapman; she was working on the last one, and had cut them all cross-sectionally, seeds and all. It was a reform that Evelyn would have to bring in. Mr Henry would be instructed in the correct way to prepare cucumber sandwiches. And where was Mr Henry when he was needed?

Mr Henry, exhausted, was hiding in the cellar. He lay on sacking, his heart pumping, and his breath short. He must look, he thought, like some ghastly Victorian allegorical painting — *The Decline of Scholarship* or some such. He knew what had to be done. To assist with the food, with the supply into the tent of constant foodstuffs, to sit at the high table with Mrs Covington, to worry about the future, about . . . about . . .

5

'An Indian summer evening.'

'Indeed, Mr Henry.'

Mrs Covington sat in the middle seat of seven ranged behind the long table raised on a platform of beer crates. To her left were Mr Henry, Julia, and an empty seat for Roland. On her right sat Evelyn, the Reverend Purvis, and James. Before them, the seven tables were crowded, storm lanterns lit on each.

'But I think,' Mrs Covington continued, drawing her shawl about her shoulders, 'that it will grow cold. Every year I recognise fewer and fewer of these people. The children grow up and their parents grow older.'

'Ah, one wishes time could stop.'

'Well yes — one can wish. Fat lot of good that will do. Have you seen to everyone, Evelyn?'

'Yes. There is beer and cider for the men and lemonade for the women and children.'

'There are some girls there — surely they are drinking beer?'

'I hope not.'

'Keep your eyes on the situation. The married women may have cider. Or sherry, I suppose. But don't let the girls get drunk. God knows what will happen. I often think that girls in the country are far worse than those in the town. It must be the proximity to the animals or something.'

'Mother — quiet. Someone will hear you.'

'All right. Mr Henry, slip to the house and bring back some sherry. What else have we got? For us?'

'Wine,' said Evelyn.

'I think I'd rather have beer,' said Mrs Covington.

'You can't have *beer*.'

'I can have what I like, Evelyn. This is my house, or rather, my tent, and *my* beer. Mr Henry, before you go, please get me a small glass of beer from Mr Parchman. Don't look so effortlessly miserable, Evelyn. We had better get events moving, I think. Mr Purvis — would you do the usual for us? Thank you.'

It was the duty of the Reverend Purvis to open the Michaelmas celebration each year by paying tribute to the generosity of Mrs Covington in allowing her lovely house and garden to be used for these annual festivities and how it was his privilege to have been present at — and here he would turn to Mrs Covington — and say 'How many years is it now?' and she would respond, 'Too many.'

As she did now. And it brought the same

easy laugh from the tables below, where the men itched to sink their first pints of the night, the children looked slightly restive and bored, and the women waited to get up and go and load plates for their families from the buffet ranged on trestle tables at one side of the marquee. Mr Parchman stood ready to do his duty, with one arm slung easily over the barrel of beer, as if it was the shoulder of an old friend.

'Indeed, what a pleasure it is to see so many old friends, and some new ones too in the shape of these dear children, though we must not forget also those who are no longer able to join us, those who have, as we say, gone before us to glory . . . ' So the annual speech of this unaggressively agnostic Anglican clergyman proceeded down its set lines. He ended with a short grace, which seemed to combine thanks for the fruits of the earth with a mild disbelief in their possible Provider.

Mr Henry returned with three bottles of sherry. Evelyn drank water. The tenants and their families ate and drank and gradually the noise in the tent grew and grew.

'It has turned out jollier than I anticipated, thank God,' said Mrs Covington.

James leaned forward, speaking across the Reverend Purvis and Evelyn. 'Grandma, I hope you don't mind but we brought the gramophone over from the house. We thought you might like some music.'

'Music?' said Evelyn.

'Yes. Why not? What sort of music?' said Mrs Covington.

'Oh no.'

'Don't be so stuffy, Evelyn. Let them have their music. We had ours.'

'I didn't,' said Evelyn indignantly.

'No — I suppose you didn't. But I thought that your husband — '

'Excuse me,' said Evelyn, 'I'm going back to the house.' She stood up.

'Whatever's the matter?' said Mrs Covington. She knew she should not have mentioned Evelyn's late husband but the man had been dead for God knows how many years.

'I have a headache and it will certainly not be aided by music.' Evelyn made her way along the backs of their chairs and stepped down. She went through the rear flap of the marquee. Her back disappeared into the evening gloom.

So, a little later, they had music. Some of the children began to dance in the space between the top table and the others. The girls jived together, their faces adopting masks of high seriousness. The older boys sat lumpishly self-conscious; only a couple of small ones capered about, mimicking the girls.

In her room, windows and curtains shut, Evelyn sat on the edge of her bed, the palms of her hands pressed to her ears to shut out the faintest vestige of that far, braying row. She sat and rocked forward and back and she wept, for the first time in many years.

★   ★   ★

It was almost eleven. Mrs Covington had made a dignified exit an hour earlier. Shortly after, released from their obligations to their landlord (as Mr Henry had wittily said, 'You could not really be a landlady in the country, could you?'), the tenants had gone quickly enough. Only one remained: at a table, his face sideways on the soiled cloth, a bubble forming between his oddly pursed lips, one of the farmers' sons slept in a deep alcoholic stupor.

James and Julia stood facing each other in the space made for dancing. On the turntable the same tune, *Night and Day*, for the third time. James had just put it back on. A violin began to state the melody, and they began to dance again.

He held her quite closely to him. The

fingers of her right hand rested lightly on his shoulder, he held her left hand almost to his cheek, his other hand rested in the small of her back and the silk of her dress moved his hand over her skin. They danced slowly, hardly more than circling the same spot of worn grass.

'Julia?'

'Yes.'

His face came forward as she spoke. He kissed, or half-kissed her, missing her mouth as she turned her head away.

'What?' She sounded uncertain. Her eyes had widened.

'I'm sorry.'

'What?'

'I didn't mean . . . '

'Didn't mean what?'

'I mean . . . '

'Did you want to kiss me just then?'

'Yes. I think so.'

'I'm sorry. I didn't know. I looked away just as you tried.'

They had stopped dancing. The record ended. Her fingers squeezed his almost unnoticeably. They kissed. He had never known any sensation so wonderful. A great warmth flowered in his body. When they drew apart, he knew that his life and feelings would never be the same again. He felt such a marvellous tenderness towards this girl that —

'Hello kiddies. What're you up to then?'

The voice cut into the pure silence. In an instant Julia had withdrawn her hand and stepped back from James.

Roland was standing between the marquee flaps. 'Don't mind me,' he said and walked unsteadily past them to the beer barrel, sweeping a half-pint glass off a table as he went. He bent down and held the glass under the barrel's spigot and helped himself. 'Thank Christ there's some left,' he murmured. He straightened up and turned back.

'Where'd she go then? Good health.' He drank deeply.

Julia had gone. James had not even noticed in the shock of seeing his father.

'Bloody good party this,' said Roland. 'No bugger left.'

6

Julia had hardly slept. Last night she had fled straight to her room. After perhaps half an hour, she had heard her uncle's voice, rumbling and indistinct down in the hall. James's voice then said clearly, 'I'll just go to bed, if you don't mind. Not for me.'

'Warra na na boy. Man,' said the rumble, then sweetly wheedling, but now also clear, 'Come on. Just the one.'

The two of them had gone into the library. Roland kept his whisky there, on a tray; the bottle was frequently replaced. She had heard the door shut; then silence came again as if a thick blanket had been placed over the house.

Later, she lay awake and imagined James in his uniform, holding a glass of whisky in one hand, a cigarette in the other. Then he was holding her in the marquee. The music had not ended. Then it had and he was being awkward. He kissed her. Then that awful voice spoke behind them. She broke stupidly away from James, pulling her hand from his and, seconds later, running off in a panic, like a stupid little girl. What was she feeling now? The tune began again in her head. They

275

danced. She felt his hand on the small of her back; her fingers rested on the blue felt-like material of his tunic. Its bright brass buttons shone. The music stopped again. James was kissing her once more. The voice spoke. She broke away. She ran over the damp grass and into the house and across the tiled hall and up the stairs and along the gallery. Her mother's voice came querulously from behind her door, saying, 'Is that you, Julia? What time is it?'

She had made some sort of reply. Had she slammed her door? Yes. No. Over and over, she rehearsed the events in her head. The earliest part of the evening was rapidly gone over and dispensed with. Then there was the music. Their first awkward steps. Then all was telescoped rapidly into the compass of that three-minute guitar and violin gramophone record. The dance. The kiss. The voice. The break away. Hall. Gallery. Mother. Door. Here, now, going over it all again and again in the dark — was this what was meant by love? Was this the beginning of those feelings hinted at in the poems and stories? And why had it got to be James? He was her cousin. That was all right. It must be. He was going back to camp. She wouldn't see him again. He was bored here. He wouldn't want to come back. People married their first cousins.

The royal families in Europe had always done it. She smiled bleakly into the darkness. What did it matter if they were in love? Then she was frightened because she had said that word in her head. A word that was in all the poetry that Mr Henry had given her to read over the past five years. A word that was never spoken otherwise. A word that, she knew, her mother would regard as 'dirty' outside the confines of a book. None of these people had ever loved anybody in their stupid lives. And they had shut her up in this house for so long that she no longer knew how to behave. Or, rather, she knew how to behave like a character in a book, a paper ghost; she knew precisely how to say their words, the words of people who didn't exist, had never existed, would never exist. The books — more precisely, the men and women in them — had comforted her. But they were not life. Mr Henry had lived his whole life worshipping these objects. What had he learned from them? Julia thought of Mr Henry; of the fussiness of his hands at the table last night as he forked food into that lipless mouth with its teeth like yellow-grey pumice stones. She thought of him reading, a spider's-web thin thread of spittle spooling down to make a tiny darker spot on the lapel of his navy-blue blazer. And of his muffled whinny when he was amused by what he was reading.

James stood in the marquee. She ran away. She ran back to him. Uncle Roland appeared between the marquee flaps. Disappeared. Appeared again. Had he seen them? Had he seen that crucial moment? Would he tell her mother? Was she to be watched and commented upon all the time from now on? To become a character with them, to share her grandmother's calculated eccentricities, her mother's sourness and denial of life, of sex, of any interruption of her cosy world by *the* world?

He was going back to camp tomorrow.

Julia thought that she was condemned to be tormented all night by this repetition of memories, but in the end she did fall asleep and dreamed of nothing in particular until morning.

★ ★ ★

'There are rumours of dissatisfaction in Poland and Hungary.'

'You know the rules, Mr Henry. No news on Sunday,' said Mrs Covington.

'Oh. Because we missed yesterday's bulletin — I thought it might please.'

'Well it doesn't. Evelyn, did you see what Mr Purvis's wife was wearing this morning. It

278

was quite unsuitable. How old is she?'

Mrs Covington was having a fine time discussing the shortcomings of the vicar's wife and the drunken habits of the younger of the Parchman boys. Then, noticing how glum Mr Henry was looking, she relented and turned to him.

'There, there, Mr Henry. You know that we all positively adore your news bulletins. Prepare a bumper one for lunch tomorrow and we shall all be absolutely delighted. Won't we?'

'Um,' Roland murmured.

Evelyn and Julia said nothing.

And James was thinking about last week at camp.

★ ★ ★

'You're a fucking pig. That's what you are. You're a fucking little fat piggy. What are you? Get down on the floor. Go on. That's where pigs belong. Fucking down. Now pig — act like a pig. Go on. Pig. Pig. Look at this. Get your nose on the floor, pig. Your fucking snout. Grunt, pig. Grunt.'

Poor, pudgy Aircraftman Second Class Miller, on his hands and knees, lowered his head so that the tip of his nose almost touched the floor.

'Lower.'

As soon as the nose actually touched the floor, Sergeant Phillips, in one concerted, almost balletic motion, planted his right foot on Miller's backside, pushing him sprawling forward, while with his left hand Phillips deftly overturned Miller's bed.

'Right. Now do it properly. Why the fuck are you lot smirking? You're all as fucking bad. Get this place cleaned up. Right now.'

What would the people round his grandmother's table think if they could hear Sergeant Phillips screaming and bellowing? Julia was smiling at him. A couple of the men were married and a couple more had pictures of girlfriends, but the rest of them were virgins, or as good as. Fucking virgins, as Phillips put it oxymoronically. But then, his favourite word was never used for the one function it actually described. But that desire — losing one's virginity — was one crossed with terror and disgust after the film on VD they had been shown last week. Those huge, close-up magnifications of sex organs, male and female . . . He had never seen it before. He couldn't believe that Julia was made like that. It was quite impossible. The doctor had said it — 'Enough to put you off for life, eh boys?'

The one thought that kept them all going

was that they would never have to see Phillips again. He was retiring this year, he informed them, and he was going to go out with a 'fucking bang'. They were going to win the Drill Cup for him that year, 'by hook or by fucking crook'.

On the day of the competition, it didn't seem to James that their squad was conspicuously worse or better than any of the others. But by some careful and sentimental stage-management by the officers, it appeared that the soon-to-be-retired sergeant's squad had won. That night, led by Sergeant Phillips, they all roared off in a truck to the nearby town. The theatre was presenting a Service show called *Soldiers in Skirts*. As they got down from the truck, the sergeant, already reeking of whisky, embraced each of them in turn, saying tearfully to each uniformed man, 'Best fucking squad I ever had. Best fucking squad.' And when poor Piggy Miller got down, last of all of course, the sergeant advanced terrifyingly on him, but threw his arms round him, his voice now a tear-filled mumble, 'And you was the best of all in the end, Piggy. Best of the fucking lot.'

After the show — which the sergeant slept through — he insisted that James and the others accompany him to the pub across the road from the theatre. There he found he had no money, so they treated him and told him, quite truthfully, that he was the best sergeant they had ever had.

They hadn't been in the pub for more than ten minutes when some of the actors came over from the theatre.

'Sarg — from the show,' said one of the boys.

The actors stood in a knot at the bar. Their faces looked abnormally pink or sandy from stage make-up. They were led by a burly sergeant with wig-like grey hair cut *en brosse*.

'Arrgh. The show.' Sergeant Phillips wheeled round and lurched towards his fellow non-commissioned officer, shouting. 'Best fucking show I ever seen. Wonderful fucking acting. Could've sworn you were all fucking women.'

'What are you smiling at, Jamie?' said his father. 'Let us all in on the secret.'

'Nothing. Nothing.'

His grandmother laughed.

'Leave the boy alone, Roland,' she said.

★   ★   ★

It was late afternoon. James and Julia sat on the window seat, dealing cards in turn on to a game of Patience that had already run through too many hands. Their conversation was limited to remarks on the cards, on the difficulty in 'getting out' at all this afternoon. The only other sounds were the dull tuck-tuck of the library clock and the papery flick as Evelyn every now and then turned the pages of the *Illustrated London News*. Every time this sound came, Julia would roll her eyes and grimace like a monkey, and James would reply with a broad grin and a slight shake of his head.

'Well, that's it,' said Julia after another unsuccessful game. 'That's enough of cards for today.' She paused and then looked straight at James as she said, 'Would you like to go for a walk, James?' She frowned at him and mouthed a silent *Yes*.

'A walk — where?' said her mother immediately.

'Just out.'

There was silence. Evelyn had given in on one front — that Julia must sometimes be allowed to leave the confines of the house and garden — but she had sought to surround any outing with conditions and caveats.

'I really don't think that the village is quite the thing, Julia. Especially after the last time. It is one thing for James — but not for you, not immediately after church. So where else?'

'We can go across the fields and round the Old Manor.'

'It will be getting dark soon.'

'Not for ages. And we'll only be a little while.'

'James has to go back to camp early tomorrow.'

'We'll be back before dark.'

★ ★ ★

They walked slowly back in the dusk. She had asked him about his training. He had given her a sanitised account. It was a pity in a way. He would have liked to tell somebody about how the constant physicality of the life induced a tiredness at the end of each day that was pleasant in its own way, and how uncomplicated the language of the barrack room was, with its farts and food and football and sexual speculation, and how the constant repetition of the 'f' word, deployed in all possible connections as verb, adjective or adverb, though rarely as a noun, came to have a mad sort of poetry about it.

She put her hand in the crook of his arm. The house was almost in sight; she could feel it, waiting round the bend of the road, behind the screen of elms. They were at the stile at the end of the footpath across the fields. James clambered over first, and held out his hands to help. She waved them aside and jumped down. She landed so close that she fell against him and his arms instinctively held her. She turned her face up to his and he did not let go. They kissed for the second time, the passion of the previous night already replaced by the relish and comfort of experience.

They walked on easily then, hand in hand. The glassed cupola and upper windows of the house came into view over the garden trees as they rounded the corner.

'What are we going to do?' Her voice was so low that he thought he had misheard what she said.

'James.' Her fingers squeezed his. 'What are we going to do?'

★ ★ ★

'Shouldn't take long,' said Roland. He was in his mother's room. She sat at the bureau. She was counting the year's rents. On the desk were pound and ten shilling notes in tottering piles, made higher by their used and crumpled states, a much lower mound of clean white five pound notes that had obviously been carefully saved for Michaelmas, and piles and piles of silvery half-crowns and florins, thin high columns of shillings and sixpences and puddles of brown coppers.

'I'll drop James back to his camp, then double back to Shrewsbury, pay in the rent, and come on straight back here.'

'I wish you were going to the bank first. I don't like to think of all this money floating about in your car.'

'They don't open till ten. I have to have James at his camp by eight at the latest. You don't want the boy on a charge for being AWOL.'

'Yes — but you will look after it?' she said for perhaps the fourth time that evening.

'What do you think?'

'You'll pay it in at once — as soon as you reach Shrewsbury?'

'No. I'll spend it all on chorus girls and champagne.'

'Don't joke about this thing,' she said. 'Money is not easily come by now and things are rather tight at the moment.'

'You've been saying that for the last twenty years, Mama.'

'That doesn't make it any the less true.'

★ ★ ★

As they drove, James said, 'Our drill sergeant retires this year. He's a funny old chap. He was absolutely awful to us for a long time. Then he softened up after training was done.

286

What do you think he'll do when he leaves? What do people like that do out of the service?'

'They disappear,' said his father. 'They shrink back into life and they're no longer terrible or terrifying. He'll shed his uniform and he'll look smaller. And he'll be smaller. He's probably been in the mob all his life, poor bastard. He'll get taken on as a jobsworth somewhere, I don't doubt.'

'What's a jobsworth?'

'Oh, you know — 'More than my job's worth, squire' — type. Nightwatchman. Commissionaire. Something like that.'

They came to the T-junction where the camp was marked by a road sign pointing west.

'Just up there, isn't it? I won't take you all the way. Wouldn't do to see you roll up in a flash car, would it? I know all about it. You have to be the same as the others. Only fair. Okay? Best of luck, old son. Sorry about me and your mother. Write to her or something. All right — you'd better cut along.'

They shook hands awkwardly, and James got out of the car. He hoisted his kitbag and set off for camp.

Roland sat for a few minutes. To go back north to Shrewsbury he should have turned round and gone back the way he came.

Instead he gently eased the car forward to the junction and turned the car to the east. In his rear view mirror he could see, far up the road to the west, James walking briskly towards the camp.

The car gathered speed. If he put his foot down he could be in London for lunch and a drink.

PART FOUR

1

Mr Henry reported on more riots in Poland. Rumours of unrest in East Germany and Hungary. The killing of six soldiers by terrorists in Cyprus. His remark that the sole consolation would appear to be that the Bolshevik empire seemed to be in danger of collapse went unnoticed. Mrs Walters rarely spoke, he knew, but even Mrs Covington, who usually interrupted or tested him with questions, was silent.

She sat bolt upright. Every now and then she raised her fork, with the same scrap of lamb and crushed peas, almost to her mouth, only to lay it down again, untouched, glancing sharply every now and then out of the open door into the hall.

He tried to tempt her with an interesting murder case. A woman was accused of smothering two children on some squalid barge on the Thames. The interest was that she was the daughter of a solicitor and her husband was a black man.

'How awful,' said Evelyn.

Mrs Covington looked at her watch for the third time in five minutes.

'What time is it?' she asked irritably.

'Twenty-five past two,' said Mr Henry.

'It is right then,' said Mrs Covington.

'Is something the matter?' said Evelyn.

'He should be back by now,' said Mrs Covington.

'Who — Roland? I think we should know better than to worry about his timekeeping. Heavens — he could be away for hours.'

'No, he promised he would be straight back this morning.'

'Mother — we're talking about Roland.'

'Yes.' Mrs Covington seemed all at once to regain her composure. 'Mr Henry,' she said, 'have you lost your voice?'

'No. I was telling everyone about this dreadful murder . . .'

'Let it rest until tomorrow. I'm sure we shall enjoy the murder tomorrow.' She rose from her chair. 'Julia,' she said, 'I wonder if I might see you for a few moments in my room. In five minutes?'

★ ★ ★

Julia went upstairs. Her mother had looked quite upset. The natural order of things had been disturbed. Julia felt quite proud and excited to have been chosen this once.

Her grandmother stood at the bureau.

Papers were strewn all over it and on the floor beneath.

'Shut the door, child. Sit down. On the bed. That's it.' Mrs Covington sank into the chair in front of the bureau, turning sideways as she did so, running a hand through her white hair, looking at Julia in a new way.

'The first thing that must be made clear . . . ' she began, then stopped. She went on after a moment. 'I want to ask you, Julia, to do me a small favour. I don't want you to say anything about it to your mother. Or Mr Henry. Or anyone. Not that there is anyone else. It is all so tedious, but I don't want to worry them needlessly. Not that there is anything to worry about. It's just that . . . And I certainly don't want you to regard yourself as deceitful in withholding anything from your mother.'

'I understand,' said Julia. But she wondered if the old woman's mind was beginning to wander. She certainly appeared older all at once, with shadows in her temples and a distracted, powerless air about her.

'You know of a telephone?'

'Sorry?'

'A telephone. Is there one in the village?'

'There's a public box at the side of the green.'

'A public telephone?' Mrs Covington spoke

as if this was a dangerously revolutionary instrument, and Julia wondered once more how much of her grandmother's ignorance of the world was real and how much was affectation. For the first time, and to her own astonishment, Julia realised that she was looking at her grandmother as an old woman, a rather pathetic old woman — not as the hierarchic totem with severe face and severer tongue who, indestructible and immortal, walked briskly about the house, her hands shooting out in gestures of command and supervision.

'It is a matter of business,' said Mrs Covington. 'Personal business.' She hesitated. She stirred a hand listlessly in the papers on the desk. Then she finally decided to divulge her thoughts. 'You must ring the bank in Shrewsbury. I shall give you the number. You must ask for Mr Hinton, the manager. Hinton. You are to say that you are my granddaughter, that I am indisposed but that I need some details of my farm account. You must ask him if any money has been deposited in the farm account at any time today. In particular, the exact sum of one thousand, four hundred and twenty-seven pounds, seventeen shilling and sixpence. That is all I need to know.'

'Beauty is truth, truth beauty' — that is all
Ye know on earth, and all ye need to know.

The quotation, in Mr Henry's 'poetry' voice, came into Julia's head. And a sudden picture of James, seen through the side window at the front door, in his blue uniform, the lighter blue of the sky behind him.

'Is that clear?'

Yes, it was perfectly clear.

Julia went downstairs. In the library she told her mother that she had to go to the village to make a telephone call for her grandmother. Her mother thought this absurd — she would do it herself. She marched out of the room and Julia heard her mount the stairs, and go along the gallery . . . In a brief while she was back. 'You had better go then,' she said shortly. 'Have you change? Here's a shilling in copper. Do you know how to work the thing?'

Her mother accompanied her to the gate. She glared suspiciously towards the village.

'Just the telephone, Julia. Do you understand? Just the telephone and straight back.'

A strange afternoon. As she walked to the red telephone box outside the post office on the opposite side of the green, the sun appeared between the rain clouds so that a blade of light followed her across the grass and overtook her, crossing the still water of the pond.

She came to the box just as an elderly man on a bicycle passed. He raised his hat and the front wheel wobbled.

She got through to the bank.

The manager was delicate voiced and prissily mannered. He asked Miss Walters to hold on while he summoned his clerk. There was a murmuring of voices, the turning of pages of, presumably, large leather-bound ledgers. No, there had been no deposits today. There had been a recent withdrawal. Of three hundred and fifty pounds.

'Thank you,' said Julia.

'Thank *you*. Please convey my best regards to your grandmother,' said the manager.

* * *

Mrs Covington had re-composed herself while Julia was away in the village. Roland had promised to come straight back after paying in the money, but Roland was Roland, after all — always late. Her colour improved in the dressing-table mirror. When she heard what Julia had to say her face changed for a moment to an ashy white. Then *Courage*, she said to herself. *Courage*. It could not be

296

much worse, but it could be worse. Her son had left her a little in the account.

For the next three days, Julia repeated her visits to the telephone box. It took the greatest will-power on Mrs Covington's part not to send the child out as early as practicable in the morning. But the thought of Roland making the deposit right on the deadline of three-thirty in the afternoon, leaving her to guess for the rest of the day and evening and night, that was even more unbearable. So, she waited through the afternoons, poring over her papers, pulling this one to her, pushing this one away, knowing all the while the tale they told. It was not until Friday that she gave up hope and asked Julia if she would be so kind as to send Evelyn to her room.

She did not notice, until too late, that Julia remained in the room all through the subsequent meeting. Evelyn sat on the edge of the bed. Mrs Covington sat at the bureau. Julia must have been by the door, sitting on that delicate bamboo chair that seemed hardly strong enough to bear anyone's weight. Perhaps that had contributed to the girl's impression of invisibility.

Evelyn would not take well what she had to say — Mrs Covington drew some satisfaction from that thought.

She told her the facts. Roland had had charge of the money on Monday morning. It had not been paid into the bank that day, or any day since. There had been no word from Roland. It must be assumed, after a week, that he had made off with the money. He had also cashed a cheque, which he must have forged, for a large amount.

Somehow, saying all of this lightened Mrs Covington's mood. A trouble shared is a trouble halved — and why shouldn't Evelyn be worried for a change?

'It appears, in short, that we are ruined,' Mrs Covington said almost cheerfully.

'I know it's an awful amount,' said Evelyn, blinking, 'but there must be some rational explanation. Roland must be found and made to disgorge. It's ridiculous that he should carry our money around with him like this.'

'Can you suggest how we do that? I would remind you that this represents a whole year's rent, plus a considerable amount of cash on top.'

'If he has taken the money — if he has stolen the money then he must pay it back. Or risk the consequences. Meanwhile we are hardly ruined. We have the farms, the estate, the house. We can borrow against those until Roland pays back the money.'

'Let me explain,' said Mrs Covington

patiently. 'The farms are mortgaged to the hilt. So is this house. All the rents go on repaying the debts that we have. We live on very little, Evelyn. My pension. Yours. We can get by for a little time. And then . . . '

'Things can't be that bad. They can't possibly be. If they are, we shall just have to sell one of the farms to raise capital.'

'I have just told you, Evelyn — we do not own the farms. We do not. The banks own the farms. With the pensions, we can struggle on for a while. I did hope,' she said wistfully, 'that I might have seen my time out here.'

'For God's sake — stop it. We must find Roland at once.'

'How?'

'Set the police on him.'

'Your brother? Half of it will have gone already to pay his debts, the other half will go down his throat. And if we do get the police to look for him and the news gets around that we are — to put it crudely — broke, all hell will break loose.'

'Well then, what is to be done? What? We can't just leave. We can't not live here. What about Julia?' It was then that they both became aware that Julia was sitting by the door. 'Julia — go downstairs please and see to the, to the . . . '

'Leave her,' said Mrs Covington. 'She's

heard it all. She has to know.'

'And Mr Henry. He will have to go. Now,' said Evelyn.

'Shush, Evelyn. Mr Henry may not be so easily got rid of; it may indeed be in our interests not to get rid of him. He has a small pension, I believe. And some savings. Not enough for him to set up on his own, but enough for him to perhaps row in with us in some way. He was hoping to buy an annuity, I believe. He must be somehow gently dissuaded from the plan. His capital may enable us to weather the storm. Separately we sink; together we may just about swim.'

'And what about Julia?'

'Ah, Julia.'

They both turned to Julia, but she had already left the room.

★ ★ ★

'And now you're proposing to cheat poor Mr Henry. You talk about Uncle Roland, but you're as bad.'

'We are trying to survive, Julia. You stupid child. Do you want to go out to work? To work in some office. Or factory? No, of course not.'

'I will. If it's necessary.'

'If it is *necessary*? What do you think life is?

I've protected you all this time from making my mistakes. An expensive education has been paid for. A private tutor. And what have you learned?'

'It hasn't been protection though, has it? All this nonsense about innocence. Mermaids and Kings and Queens of England and poetry and the Empire and nice young ladies — you've never really wanted to know at all what I might like or need. Look at when I started — '

'Don't be disgusting. I wanted you to be different. Now I see — oh, I see — that you are determined to be just like all the others. All right — see how you survive. Do you think you'll be any different? Give you a war or two and having the choice of deciding how to live your life taken away from you. Give you a marriage and a child. You think you love this boy, James, don't you? Perhaps you do in some coltish immature way. But he's your cousin, your first cousin. I thought that wasn't right. It's not right. But now, I really couldn't care less. Go ahead and make the same mistakes I did. I really don't care.'

'What mistakes? You sound horrible. Was I one of your mistakes? You married Daddy. You loved him. You must have done.'

'We all *love*.'

301

'And you still loved him when he died.'

'He didn't *die*.'

'What do you mean?'

'Your father killed himself.'

2

22nd October 1956
Dearest Julia,

I have heard about this awful thing to do with my father and Grandmother's money. It is absolutely dreadful. I didn't have any idea. Grandmother wrote to me asking if I knew where Dad was. When I wrote and said I didn't know, she wrote back telling me why she was trying to find out. He must have gone mad. But, whatever he is or isn't, he is still my father. Another but — and a big one, I'm afraid — is that I don't see how I can possibly spend my next leave with you at the Round House. My father's conduct, if it's as bad as I've been told, is unforgivable, and I would hardly be welcome. If I were, I wouldn't deserve to be and I should feel awful and ashamed. It is such a pity that I shall not be able to see you.

It may all be academic. Leaves haven't actually been cancelled yet, but there's a rumour that they might be. We — that is the other boys and I — are all very confused by the situation at the moment. I do agree with my father in this, at least, when he said that it would be wrong to use force against a country that has not actually attacked us and just because we think historically that we somehow still own it. Some of the older men, who were due for demob, have heard another rumour that they may be held over and not be able to leave the service on their due date. I sympathise with them no end. My father may be a fool, or worse, but he did say once that the purpose of the young is not to reproduce the errors of the old; they must rebel and do something new and all of their own. He fought in the war, after all, so should know something about it. If we have to fight, I suppose we shall, but it does seem such a shabby cause — don't you agree? Please agree. I know your grandmother and mother won't, but you don't have to agree with them just out of your regard for them.

Must dash,

Love,

James

23rd October 1956

My dear James,

We must, we must see each other.

Julia started a fresh piece of paper three times with that one sentence. Each time, she stared at it, shook her head, and screwed the paper into a ball and threw it into the corner by the waste-paper basket. The three lay there now, the latest still faintly rustling as its creases partially reopened.

She wanted to write to James, but the thing that her mother had told her kept sweeping aside everything else in her head.

She stared at the white paper in front of her on the desk, and she thought of that winter's day when her mother had called her downstairs and told her what was wrong. What forever would be wrong. Her father had died suddenly. There was nothing to be done. Then that other earth-and-stone-coloured morning a few days after, when she had stood in the churchyard with the few other people motionless as statues above her. The words that the priest droned promised eternity, but the rattle of gravel on the coffin lid was the end of rhetoric. She hadn't cried then, but later, on her own. Even then, those years ago, her mother's words had been unaccountably cruel.

She said that Julia's father had failed in his duty to them by dying. He had let the whole family down. Her mother reminded Julia constantly that her family had never approved of the match. If he had become an officer all would have been well. Their social situation would have improved. He would never have been put in the position of suffering such a stupid and unnecessary accident. But then Julia would hear her mother saying, with a cold sort of pride, to almost strangers, 'My husband died of injuries he sustained in the war.' And for Julia, the picture of her father carried forward from childhood had been subsumed over the years within the larger, the generalised idea of the Hero. This was the man who served in her dreams to explore, to do battle, to stand in doorways, to talk softly and indistinctly to someone just out of sight — the hero she sought in novels and poems, the hero whose voice sang sometimes from one or two of the red-and-blue-labelled records in the sitting room.

Now her mother had killed the Hero.

Julia at last began to write her letter again . . .

At the end of your last letter you write of my regard for my mother and grandmother, and for, I suppose, poor Mr Henry too. I don't think that regard is the right word, and I don't think that 'regard' is any longer unqualified for any of them.

Life here has become truly absurd. Mr

Henry has been told that he really must ease off from his domestic duties — after he had been used almost as a servant for the past few weeks. My mother informed him, in a very 'madamly' fashion, that it was time that 'Julia's education was taken in hand again, with a view to her future.' This was said in front of me. I think she is quite mad. I refused point blank. I said that my future was my own responsibility. I was going to say that I didn't see how the education given me so far had fitted me for any conceivable future. It would have been very clever sounding, but Mr Henry was still in the room and I did not want to hurt him.

Oh James, I feel such a prisoner here. You are the one true thing I have met with and you won't come here. Everything that was good about this place is now poisoned by my mother. Even India is spoilt for me. I left it when I was only very young, but I remember it. The heat and light and smells and people and my ayah are all still in my heart. But all Grandmother and Mother can do now is to hate India. I think they hate everything. Write back, dear James, as soon as ever you can.

If you really feel you cannot come to the house, perhaps we could meet elsewhere.

You are not so far away. I looked up
Credenhall on the map and it is not so very
far. Well — it might as well be on the other
side of the moon for all I can get there. But
I'm sure I can get away for a while at least.
Of course Mother will kick up a fuss, but
they can hardly keep me locked up for ever,
can they?

Until we meet,
All love
Julia.

Julia's previous letters had all been posted by
Mr Henry, on his morning visits to the
village. He had been under her strict
instructions not to mention them to anyone.
It was all, he thought, rather exciting, like the
kind duenna or nurse who aids the cause of
true love in novels and plays. And, in a way,
he had undertaken the task to spite the ladies.
But things had somehow, lately, begun to get
a little better. He thanked God that there had
not been a position available at his cousin's
school. He seemed to have won a reprieve
from Mrs Covington. She had even said,
mysteriously, tantalisingly, that perhaps the
household should draw closer still; that 'in
these perilous times' they should be more of a
community, more of a partnership. She could
say no more at the moment. He had nodded,

in perfect understanding and complete ignorance.

Even the news he brought to the lunch table seemed to be getting better. True, Julia had barked her defiance at some interpretation by her mother, and even got up from the table once or twice and stormed out. But this, he supposed, was something that young ladies did. They did it in novels when the plot demanded. In real life it was probably more to do with hormones and burgeoning sexuality and all those things he did not care to think about too deeply.

In the past few days alone, there had been dramatic and cheering news. True, the endless rounds of talks about Suez continued between governments, with even the Indians suggesting a compromise plan. ('The Indians?' Evelyn had snorted. 'How ridiculous.') There had been more murders in Cyprus, but to balance that the British had captured a Mau Mau field marshal in Kenya.

He read out with relish the description of the field marshal.

'I quote: 'When captured he was dressed in roughly tailored — ''

'Tailored?' Evelyn gave her sharp, derisory laugh.

'' — tailored animal skins; he wore a cap and jacket of leopard skin, a coat of antelope skin with a monkey-skin collar, and short trousers of antelope skin. He also wore some army-type clothing and a leather jerkin. A police officer said that a special effort had been made to capture Kimathi during Princess Margaret's visit.''

'What a splendid idea,' said Evelyn.

'You sound as if he's some sort of wild animal,' said Julia. 'A piece of game.'

'That's exactly what he is. An animal.'

'You laugh at his clothes. What else is he supposed to wear?'

'Exactly.'

'You wear a fox around your neck,' said Julia.

'Ah, that is as a warning to other little foxes,' said Mrs Covington.

They all laughed, except Julia whose face went very red with suppressed tears and anger.

That was on Tuesday. By Thursday the Polish crisis appeared to have been solved, with concessions to limited reform by the Russians. But now there were demonstrations in Hungary.

'The students and workers have attempted to pull down a statue of Stalin,' Mr Henry announced.

'That is going too far,' said Evelyn.

By the next day, it appeared that a

full-scale insurrection had broken out in Budapest.

'The Poles were our allies,' said Mrs Covington. 'One has every sympathy for them. I'm not sure whose side the Hungarians were on.'

'They are fighting for freedom,' said Julia despairingly.

'Freedom is relative,' said Evelyn.

It was just then that Mr Henry wished, to his intense surprise, that all this might stop. Not the fighting in a faraway city, but this — this table, these chairs, these people sitting on them . . . It was only the autumn coming on, he thought, the shortening afternoons; it always brought on this depression.

On Saturday, the 27th of October, he announced that the fighting in Budapest continued, and that riots had broken out in the Chinese schools of Singapore. But Princess Margaret had returned from her tour of Africa in 'vivid high spirits,' to quote *The Times*.

'A beautiful girl,' remarked Mrs Covington. 'Let us hope that she has been able to put all that unfortunate Townsend business behind her.'

'She sacrificed herself for duty,' said Evelyn, looking meaningfully at her daughter.

Julia said bitterly, 'That's fine. Unlike

Daddy, you mean.'

'What are you two talking about? Be quiet,' said Mrs Covington. 'Mr Henry is trying to give us the news. What does the paper have to say about the homecoming of the Princess?'

'I can do no better than to read the report.' Mr Henry adjusted his reading glasses and began: ''A few minutes before the aircraft was due to land the Queen and the Queen Mother arrived at the royal lounge by car together. The Queen wore a deep crimson coat, with an ornament gleaming on one lapel, and her matching hat had a trimming of pink feathers. The Queen Mother wore a coat of lilac tone, and carried a silver fox stole looped across one arm.''

'You see, Julia,' said her mother triumphantly.

'Continue, Mr Henry,' said Mrs Covington.

''Women in the crowd who had spent several waiting minutes in lively and admiring discussion of these colour schemes exclaimed when Princess Margaret appeared in the open door of the Ajax and, with a smile that warmed hearts nearly a hundred yards away, began to walk down the gangway to greet all the subfusc men of name, grouped formally below. For the Princess, too, had chosen red for her coat and millinery — what some women spectators called cyclamen and others cherry red.''

'Ummm,' said Mrs Covington with deep appreciation.

'Shall I read more?' said Mr Henry.

'Please.'

''This chromatic counterpoint, if it were such, added to the gaiety of the scene set for Princess Margaret's home-coming as darkness began to close in on the airport. The crew of the Ajax lined up beneath the port wing to be royally thanked for 'an excellent flight', and then the Queen, the Queen Mother and Princess Margaret severally engaged in conversation with all the welcoming notabilities until, in spite of the chill, the tarmac 'apron' began to take on the appearance of a Royal garden party.

''The roof-top crowd were trembling from the cold before the Queen Mother and Princess Margaret, apparently oblivious of the autumnal bite, entered their car, drawn up near the Ajax gangway, and drove away towards Clarence House. The Queen left by car alone a few minutes later.''

'Bravo, Mr Henry. Well read,' said Mrs Covington. 'A wonderful illustration of how the Royal Family literally bring colour to our lives.' She sipped her tea.

'Is that the only news, Mr Henry?' said Julia.

'It is important, Julia,' her mother hissed.

'But what about the uprising in Hungary? That's more important than what the Queen wore.' Julia's voice was angry.

'What is Julia so excited about, Evelyn?'

'Hungary.'

'Oh, Hungary. How goes our Hungarian front, Mr Henry?'

Mr Henry had the uncomfortable feeling that somehow and in a rather unpleasant way they were patronising and snubbing the girl. He hurried on to Hungary.

'A new prime minister has been appointed. It seems that the Russians have given way and are preparing to withdraw. I think that matters will come to a head over the weekend.'

'Well — good news there, I think you will agree, Julia. The Bolsheviks have been alarmed, certainly. But I hardly see that they are to be trusted. Whoever this new man is, he will have to have some pretty cast-iron guarantees before he can trust that lot.'

'Won't it be marvellous, though, if the people there do win,' said Julia. 'The students and workers and freedom fighters.' Her eyes shone.

'I suppose so,' said Mrs Covington. 'Those are three classes of people I would normally detest. The lesson is, I suppose, that some

314

form of protest, some letting off of steam must be allowed, but there must be a limit. They must in the end hand power over to those most competent to wield it.'

'That's hardly democracy,' Julia protested.

'Democracy has not been a raging success, has it though, dear? Evelyn, see if there is any more hot water please.'

3

So they began to live through the most extraordinary fortnight. What became known afterwards as the Hungarian Uprising or Revolution ended in treachery and the smothering of hope, and what was already called by some the Suez Crisis sputtered and guttered out in humiliation like a huge, damp firework. These were the two most important weeks of their lives; not because of what they did, but because other people in faraway places suffered and died, and the people in the Round House were upset by this and resolved to either do something, or to do nothing.

Things went well at first.

Wonderful news — the Hungarian rising, though initially bloody, appeared to have been a success. The secret police were to be disbanded. The Russian forces were to withdraw, perhaps altogether. The people were certainly in no mood for a single Russian remaining on their soil.

'As the *Times*' editorial says,' said Mr Henry, ''Perhaps we have all become unused to good news and so expect disillusionment.''

A largish envelope arrived the next morning, for Julia. It contained a 45-rpm record, and a letter from James.

Tuesday, 30th October 1956

Dear Julia,
This is all the rage with the boys at the moment. I thought you might like to hear it. It's not as good as jazz, but it is very jolly. Listen to it — but it will probably upset everyone else down there.

I know I shouldn't say that, because everybody has been kind to me and my father treated them so rottenly — but what else can I say? You cannot know how much I think of you. We have some time to think now that we are not being run from pillar to post; life is quite easy so I have 'time on my hands — and you in my heart' as that Billie Holiday record said. Do you remember it? So, yes, I would like nothing better on earth than to be there. I sometimes think of you as that princess who was the Sleeping Beauty and I want to hack down all those spiky hedges that go around the garden and find you in the house and take you away. Can you not get away? If you stay there you will fall asleep. You are too good for that. I must go now.

I'm writing this on duty. Leave is cancelled at the moment because of this Canal business and so life is held up.

Love

James

Julia picked up the record and hurried downstairs. A minute or so later, the noise pounded out of the library.

One-two-three o'clock, four o'clock rock!
Five-six-seven o'clock, eight o'clock rock!
Nine-ten-eleven o'clock, twelve o'clock
    rock!
We're gonna rock around the clock
    tonight!

Julia had put it on for a second time and had begun to dance, jiving with an imaginary James, when she heard another noise behind her. She reached forward and turned down the volume.

'What in God's name is that?' Her mother's face was contorted with rage.

★ ★ ★

Mrs Covington could see that Evelyn was terrified by their financial situation, of the possibility of having their life at the Round

318

House brought abruptly to an end. She herself had regained some peace of mind. She did not know it, but some part of her had gone with Roland and the money. The steel had decayed to a more brittle and rusted iron. She had convinced herself that she did not want or need this place any more. She daydreamed often now of a small, warm flat. Above all, it must be warm. This year they kept the ancient heating system off for the first time in the autumn chill. Only one fire was lit, in the dining room. At night she put on a single bar of the electric fire in her room and felt guilty. These luxuries could no longer be afforded, she told Evelyn.

Winter was coming; only Mr Henry's news cheered them.

It had been a good week for the Empire. What were their small troubles compared with those with which the Forces had to contend? On the very day when the Russians had begun to leave Hungary, the Israelis had attacked Egyptian positions in the Sinai peninsula. She had a little money salted away that the children did not know about. The next day, and an ultimatum from the British and French had been rejected by Egypt. She lit an illicit cigarette. She turned on the other bar of the fire. Despite her nightdress, dressing gown and her imitation fur coat with real fur trimmings, it was cold. And then today, at last, Mr Henry had told them of the decisive stroke — the first British air raids on Egyptian airfields. She had felt exultant at lunch. The tiresome child, Julia, had bleated about how immoral it was to attack a small and defenceless country simply over a matter of economics. Where had she picked up such nonsensical ideas? To Mrs Covington, the British attack meant that the drift, the seemingly unstoppable drift away from Empire, had been stayed, and now the process of reversing that brown, sluggish tide was to start. An Egyptian frigate had been sunk. Britain — England — had once more proved everyone wrong about her ability, her resolve. Mr Henry was still ridiculously pessimistic. According to him, the United Nations were to meet to condemn the English action. The Americans had called it 'a gross error'. The Labour Party was opposing our intervention. Oh but she had dealt with the tutor in grand style!

'The United Nations, Mr Henry, are about as useful in dealing with dictators such as Colonel Nasser, as the League of Nations were in dealing with Messrs Hitler and Mussolini. The Americans are hypocrites and cowards. They only joined the last war at the latest and most convenient date for themselves. As for the Labour Party — a bunch of pansies and fellow-travellers where they are not outright Communists. We have done something, Mr Henry,' she said triumphantly. 'We have struck, for once, while the iron is hot.'

★ ★ ★

Mr Henry was confused. Was Mrs Covington beginning to lose her grip? An agreement, she had intimated, must be reached, for the future. Well, a financial agreement of some sort had been reached. She had ceased to pay him. Things were difficult, Mr Henry, she had said. Had he not his pension? If he was in difficulties too, he must explain his financial position to her and they would see what could be done. As to the housework — perhaps Mrs Fellowes from the village might be taken on again. Obviously, Mrs Covington had gone on to say, this would be to Mr Henry's advantage. And as his teaching duties were now at an end, perhaps the time had come when a small contribution from him towards the household expenses might be thought about . . .

Something was definitely wrong. When he had ventured to ask if anyone had heard from Mr Roland, she had turned a stony gaze on him. She would be pleased, she said, if he would not mention her son's name at table.

On Friday, he read to them from *The Times*:

"I think, he continued, the United States themselves can shoulder their full share of the blame in this matter. For the last four or five years in the Middle East they have been trouble makers rather than trouble abaters."

'That is quite true,' said Mrs Covington. 'Who was that?'

'Captain Waterhouse. A Conservative member.'

'Naturally.'

'And a little later — '

They were enjoying themselves fully today.

' — in reply to the carping of a Labour member, this is Sir John Smyth's reply: 'The sympathy of the House should go out to the troops in the Middle East, who are carrying out a formidable operation.' Here there were Opposition cries of 'Bring them back.'"

'Appalling.'

'The report of Sir John continues: 'He could think of nothing more lowering to the morale of British troops than to know the House was completely divided on this issue.''

'You see, Mr Henry. *Captain* Waterhouse. *Sir* John Smyth. These are the sort of men we have. To set against that rabble.'

'And Mr Nehru has complained of

322

'Britain's naked aggression'.'

'Oh, India. India. It really is all too bad that our children turn against us in this way. Perhaps, when we have dealt with Egypt's insolence, it will put a stop to all this nonsense in the other colonies.'

'Egypt is not a colony. It has never been a colony,' said Julia.

'Pooh. You know perfectly well what I mean, Julia.'

'Don't argue with your grandmother,' said Evelyn mechanically.

'No one wants war, child. I have lived through two wars. Dreadful things happen.'

'They are not happening to us,' said Julia.

'Do you want them to?' said Mrs Covington. 'No, of course not. This, I feel, is a turning point. We are in a position where we cannot be pushed back any further. It is our duty to resist. My goodness — ' Her laugh was a harsh, dry cackle. 'What is the point in one's being good, in having one's own religion, one's civilisation superior to all others? To be cultivated, to have — ' she spread her thin hands over the white tablecloth, ' — to have all of this — if all of this is no good? If these people are to be raised above their natural state — above us — on some sentimental whim. Where will that leave us? I will tell you. A shell. A laughing-stock. That is what we shall be. No, my dear Julia, you have such a lot to learn, so many things to know.'

'I don't think I want to know what you know,' said Julia.

'Don't be insolent,' her mother barked.

'May I leave the table?'

'No.' Her mother again.

Julia sat for a moment longer, then rose abruptly. As she left the dining room, her grandmother's voice pursued her.

'Let her go, Evelyn. Where ignorance is bliss, and all that.'

'She will apologise,' her mother's voice whined upwards.

Friday, 2nd November 1956

Dear James,
The house is in a state of madness. Grandmother ranges from excessive penny-pinching and rages about extravagance to dreams of the rise of the Empire. The house is so cold, the bedrooms are freezing. I'm writing this, but I'm soon going to move down to the kitchen where at least it is a little warm. I can't listen to Mr Henry's news bulletins any more because I've been banned from the lunch table until I have apologised to them all for getting up and

walking out the other day. Oh, if I had money I would fly from here so fast. Rescue me, James, please rescue me. Please say that you don't believe in this wretched war.

Julia

Mrs Covington dreamed of India. It was like a great, brilliantly lit ballroom in her head, with sand underfoot. She was arranging Evelyn's wedding and nothing would go right. She kept explaining things to the servants and nothing would get done. Even Mr Iqbal, the chief clerk, was irredeemably stupid. Then, impossibly, because she wasn't born yet, Julia asked to help and she said to her, 'You shouldn't be here. You are not due yet.' Then her husband, Alfred, came into the room, the room that was India, and he looked very young and said that he was marrying their daughter, Evelyn. And she said to him, 'It will be getting dark soon, hadn't you better dress?' And he said, 'No one ever dreams of the dark. Did you know that? All dreams are in the day. No one ever dreams of night.' That was very true, she said. She woke up then, early, as she always did, before there was hardly any light in the sky outside, not in the crack where she let the curtains hang open because they were so thick and heavy they oppressed her and made her think she was entombed while still alive. This horrible thought had begun to haunt her this year.

★ ★ ★

News came thick and fast. On Saturday, the air force of the Egyptians was almost totally destroyed. 'Supplied to them by the Bolsheviks,' said Mrs Covington with great satisfaction. On Sunday, there were near riots and arrests in Trafalgar Square and Whitehall. 'The rioters were whipped up by our own mad and seditious Socialists,' said Mrs Covington. When Julia said that it was a free country, Mrs Covington reminded her sharply that if they had been in Hungary they would have been shot in short order. Julia reminded her that the Russians had removed their forces from Hungary and that a British Conservative government minister had resigned in protest over the Suez affair. 'Sir Winston Churchill, meanwhile,' said Mrs Covington magisterially, 'has spoken for the nation once more.'

'Even the Americans don't support us,' said Julia.

'The *Americans* — what would you expect from them?'

At lunch on Monday, Mr Henry dolefully announced to them that the Russians had gone back on their solemn word and that their tanks had once again crossed into Hungary and had encircled Budapest. Seven more British soldiers had been shot or blown up in Cyprus. Despite this appalling news, it seemed that Monday was to be Mrs Covington's finest hour.

The British were once more in action. Paratroopers had landed in Port Said; surrender terms were being discussed with the governor of the port.

'Victory is in our grasp,' said Mrs Covington to Evelyn. 'The Americans and the United Nations may gripe and complain as much as they like, the Russians may rattle their sabres, but British force of arms, going it alone, will prove them all wrong. Mr Henry, be so kind as to read out that letter from *The Times* again. The one you clipped out.'

'From?' asked Evelyn.

'A joint letter,' said Mr Henry. 'From Lord Portal of Hungerford, Marshal of the Royal Air Force; Field Marshal, Lord Alanbrooke; and Lord Cunningham of Hynd-Hope, Admiral of the Fleet. The letter — '

'Just one moment, Mr Henry,' said Mrs Covington. 'Before you read that letter, lead us in with an extract from that spineless epistle from Mr Buggerbaggage.'

'Mother!' said Evelyn.

'Mr Malcolm Muggeridge. Ah yes — I'd forgotten that.' Mr Henry tilted his head back and stared down his reading glasses at the paper. 'Here it is. 'On the one hand there is a dubious military operation, bitterly opposed by a large proportion of the population of this country — '

'Bah,' Mrs Covington interrupted him. 'Enough. Read the other letter, Mr Henry. The one from the generals. Let England be heard.'

'Yes. This is the other letter.' Mr Henry drew himself up in his chair, his voice grew louder and firmer. ' 'Now that British Forces are irrevocably committed to their task in Egypt, is it too much to ask that public argument about the rights and wrongs of Government policy in the Middle East should be postponed so as to minimise the possibly disastrous effect of the division of the country on the morale of our men? Cannot the nation unite, at least temporarily, in wishing our forces complete and speedy success in their operations?' '

'Hah. Bravo. Bravo.' Mrs Covington clapped her hands together and held them clasped to each other at such brave words.

In the library, Julia pressed her hand over her ears, to shut out the rumble of Mr Henry's voice and her grandmother's calls of ecstasy.

★ ★ ★

The following day, and the fall was complete. The 'irrevocably committed' forces were halted. They would not advance. They would withdraw as soon as a United Nations force could replace them. An unconditional ceasefire had been concluded. A few hundred British troops were clinging to a strip of land on the edge of a huge alien continent. There was nowhere for them to go but home.

Mrs Covington did not at first comprehend what Mr Henry was attempting to explain. The United States and the United Nations, in concert, had — to put it vulgarly — 'pulled the plug' on Britain and France. General Eisenhower had just won a second term as President, probably by keeping America out of the conflict. Suddenly, there was no stomach for a fight.

'But what will happen?' Evelyn asked, bewildered.

'The Egyptians will have the Canal,' he said. It was almost as if he secretly enjoyed the ladies' discomfiture. 'The Russians have succeeded in cowing their empire; ours is immeasurably weakened.'

'They have won,' said Mrs Covington. 'All the things of which I despair will come to pass. Now we will be thrown out of everywhere. We are shown to be fallible and weak; that is what happens to the weak. You don't even have to be particularly strong yourself to intimidate the weak. You simply have to have the will to do it. An Egyptian has bested us. Our Army, our Fleet, our aeroplanes are no good to us. How will that seem to others?'

There was silence around the lunch table.

Then, from the library, came the distant sounds of trumpets and drums and a bass beat.

'What is that?' said Mrs Covington.

'Julia is playing the records that James left behind,' said Evelyn.

'Jig-a-boo music,' said Mrs Covington bitterly.

* * *

On Sunday it was November the eleventh, and so Remembrance Sunday. They went to church, and the Reverend Purvis preached a disgraceful sermon. He praised the fact that 'the comity of nations has decided for the power of good, and our country has at last seen sense'. Major-General and Mrs Lowther walked out halfway through, but Mrs Covington and Evelyn and Julia sat on, grim-faced. Julia had said she would not come, then had accompanied them. It was a small price to pay for the fact that she had decided that this was the last Sunday she would ever spend with them. She had a little money in the post office. When it opened on Monday she would draw it and board the bus — to the future.

When they got back, the house was cold and gloomy. The coal Mrs Covington had bought was inferior and burned with a curiously bleak flame. Mr Henry had remained in the house to cook lunch; roast chicken and potatoes and peas. A bottle of wine was opened, but sat ill on their stomachs and in their veins. Mr Henry longed for his room; to curl under the bedclothes and read *Great Expectations* once more, his nose slowly turning frostily red where it poked out, the fingers of the book-holding hands growing cold. He tried to start a conversation, beginning, 'To look slightly on the brighter side, Mrs Covington, I saw in the newspaper yesterday that — '

'No news on a Sunday, Mr Henry,' she said

wearily. 'You know that. In fact, there will be no more news. No more news at all. What is the point? From now on, for our sort of people, all will be bad news.'

4

The house stands at the edge of the New Year. In darkness, waiting. One light shines between the gap in the curtains of an upstairs window. The winter has been severe and, to save on heating bills, Evelyn has moved into her mother's room and the two ladies now sleep in the same bed. They have reckoned that if they spend no more than two hundred pounds a year, their remaining capital should last for another ten years. This is allowing for mortgage repayments, with the hope that interest rates do not increase. Mrs Covington is in surprisingly good health. Evelyn has added three new vertical lines to her face, one at each corner of her mouth, and the other between her eyes. She tries not to, but she thinks continually of her treacherous daughter and the seducer, James. Above all her mind dwells with luxuriant hatred on her brother. He has been heard from: he sent a cheery postcard from Melbourne, saying that he had decided to make a new life in Australia and was going into business, thanking his mother for the 'seed corn' that had enabled him to make a new start, and hoping to be able to repay her one day.

Below the ladies' bedroom, framed in the kitchen window, Mr Henry looks out to the far Malverns, their tops in snow and low dark grey cloud. There is no other help in the house; he is the sole servant now. His savings have been 'invested' in the estate. He has been promised a small dividend from next year's rents. He looks forward despondently to the evening when, after the muted excitement of their evening meal, he will read a chapter of *Sorrell and Son* to them. It could be worse, he thinks, but doesn't quite know how.

★ ★ ★

Uncle Roland's estranged wife, Margaret, lives with a man who looks like a large and nervous frog. So Julia thinks, uncharitably. Julia has been living with them for several weeks. There are no children in the house, but she sleeps in what has obviously been a child's room; the pattern on the wallpaper is of constantly repeated teddybears. The first few nights she had been kept awake for a little while by the sounds of Margaret and Arthur making love. The sly knocking of what must have been the headboard of their bed against the wall frustrated her attempts to sleep.

Thankfully, for the past few nights these noises have not been repeated. She is simply not able to connect them with the middle-aged man and woman who sit around the kitchen table with her, making desultory conversation about the day's expected weather.

She thinks about those sounds again, as she walks in Kew Gardens with James. How does she know what they are? What do they mean to her? Presumably she and James will do this thing quite soon.

He looks very fine in his long uniform greatcoat. His face is bright in the cold. She supposes she loves him. She will have to, won't she? It is the bargain of life, she thinks, that in all exchanges of worlds something may be gained, but something is also certainly lost. Mermen and Mr Henry ... And her mother. Her mother has done this for her — that she cannot feel. I cannot feel, says Julia to herself, not really, not deeply. I shall go through life trying not to hurt people, but dissimulating, pretending to emotions I can't feel.

'Are you cold?' James asks with concern.

'Not really,' she says.

She slips her gloved hand into his and squeezes it gently. 'I love you,' she says, trying to believe it.

'And I love you,' he says fervently.

'Come on,' she says. 'Let's get into the warm.'

They skirt the lake with its frozen fountain. They pass along the line of heraldic beasts, that never existed in anything but imagination or stone, and mount the steps, push open the door, and enter the artificial heat of the Palm House.